Even in the days of legalized abortion there are no easy answers for a young woman who may be pregnant. Mia is an intelligent high school student living in a Stockholm suburb. Her parents are understanding, although they are too preoccupied with their own marital problems to be of help. The father of the child is willing to marry Mia even though he, too, is still a student.

For four agonizing days Mia—who is waiting for the results of a pregnancy test—thinks about what she wants to do with her life. She is shocked to discover that *her* parents married because her mother was expecting a baby—Mia. And her grandmother disturbs Mia even more when she discloses that she had been opposed to the marriage because Mia's mother was too young and did not have a career.

Slowly Mia learns that, as her grandmother expresses it, "You never understand anything in life until you're actually involved in it." Ultimately, she realizes that she must make her decision alone—and for herself.

Young men and women will find this an important book for its honesty and deep commitment to a morality as relevant today as it ever was.

BY THE SAME AUTHOR

A Room of His Own

GUNNEL BECKMAN

translated from the Swedish
by Joan Tate

THE VIKING PRESS NEW YORK

Tre veckor över tiden (Stockholm, Albert Bonniers Förlag, 1973)
Mia (London, The Bodley Head, 1974)

FIRST AMERICAN EDITION

Published in 1975 by The Viking Press, Inc.
625 Madison Avenue, New York, N.Y. 10022
PRINTED IN U.S.A.

1 2 3 4 5 79 78 77 76 75

LIBRARY OF CONGRESS CATALOGING IN PUBLICATION DATA
Beckman, Gunnel. Mia alone.
Translation of Tre veckor över tiden.
Summary: A young Swedish girl deliberates the pros and cons of having an abortion and finds it is a decision she must make alone.
[1. Abortion—Fiction] I. Title.
PZ7.B381745Mi [Fic] 74-19427

ISBN 0-670-47394-4

Mia
Alone

Mia ran up the narrow emergency stairs, slamming down the heels of her boots, the echo ringing around the dirty yellow concrete stairwell.

She took the stairs two at a time, her shoulder bag hitting the wall with a dull thump at each stride. Suddenly her heel caught in her flared pants leg and she almost lost her balance. At the last moment she grabbed the iron railing and found herself on her knees. She stayed still for a moment, listening to the thumping of her heart and her breath rasping in her throat.

There was a smell of floor-cloth and wet stone. A revolting basement-like smell.

Then she started running again—one two three . . . run . . . run . . .

God, wasn't she at the top yet? Help, only the fifth floor. What a stupid idea to race up these awful stairs instead of taking the elevator like a normal person.

But she wasn't a normal person . . . one two three . . . not normal . . . half crazy, really crazy . . . her head ached . . . the taste of beer rose in her throat in sour bubbles. God, suppose she was sick here on the stairs. She threw herself down on the bottom step of the sixth floor and remained there, her forehead against the wall. At that moment the timed light went out and she was left in the pitch dark, only the little red eye of the switch glowing mockingly at her.

Mia didn't bother to get up and switch the light on again. She stayed there, her head against the wall, enjoying the pleasant coolness of the stone surface. The blood throbbed in her cheeks and ears, but the nausea slowly retreated.

In the still darkness, her thoughts came creeping back, scratching at the door, those confused obstinate threatening thoughts that she had deliberately kept in the background almost all day, but which now rushed in and enveloped her.

If she could get to the drugstore tomorrow . . .

If she then got the results?

If it was true?

If . . . if . . . if . . . that damned *if* had been lying there like a lump of lead in her stomach for an eternity now, spreading a kind of paralysis all through her body and soul, a paralysis which stopped her from thinking and feeling and doing anything sensible.

Talk to someone—Mother, the school counselor, Jan.

But suppose it was just a false alarm—all that fuss for nothing. But of course she should have done something. Sensible people find out . . . don't just go around like a sack of potatoes. There were even tests you could do yourself.

At first she'd thought it was her usual irregularity. That

had happened often enough and eight or even ten days had gone by sometimes. She simply couldn't *understand*; that it could happen just like that! And Jan had said it was so safe. What an idiot she'd been.

Later she'd thought it was the stress of her new school, nerves and all that, but then days had gone by, rushed by, flown by. Never had days been in such a hurry to accumulate into weeks.

It was only the last ten days that she'd been really worried. It was crazy she hadn't gone then . . . after twelve days.

But she didn't have any money. And could you get that on credit? If anything should be free, then that should. Even then it wasn't all that reliable. She'd read in the evening paper about people who'd had wrong reports, people who'd at first been overjoyed and then miserable, or vice versa.

Anyway, she couldn't go to the local drugstore. Dad's cousin Kerstin worked there. Not that she'd necessarily gossip—but you could never tell. She'd know.

She ought to talk to Mother about it.

She wouldn't be angry or anything like that. But upset, of course—and disappointed. They'd had all that out ages ago, lots of times. Mia, who was such a clever and sensible girl . . .

But Mother was always busy nowadays, her job in the daytime and then her evening classes. And she seemed so depressed. That had been going on for a long time. Dad, too.

It had begun early last spring—Mia had heard them

quarreling through the bathroom wall sometimes, though she hadn't worried all that much about it then; she had worries enough of her own. And then summer had come and the new school. And then Jan.

It would really have been much better to go and see some complete outsider at some advice bureau or something. Of course, she could go to the school counselor. That's just what they were there for; they were pledged to secrecy and all that and knew exactly what you should do. If she'd still been going to her old school, then perhaps she would have done that. Mrs. Lindberg had always been awfully nice. But this new one scared her, young and pretty and confident.

It'd be hard on Mother, too, running off to confide in a strange counselor. Mother and Dad would have to know about it sooner or later.

If there was anything to know about. God, how idiotic to flap about like this when it wasn't even certain yet. It wasn't certain at all!

Ann-Margaret at her old school had been really overdue last spring and then it'd come as usual—she said it was *psychological*—that your period didn't come just because you were so hellish afraid it wouldn't. Perhaps it was the same for her? But how long could that affect you? Not forever, surely . . . twenty-three days?

No, today was the twenty-fourth. Twenty-four.

Mia shivered and suddenly realized she was icy cold all down her back, and her neck was stiff. Laboriously, she got to her feet and switched on the light. She picked up her beret, which had fallen off, and her bag, which had slid down a couple of steps. The knees of her red corduroys were dirty and one glove had vanished.

But she couldn't be bothered to look for it. The hell with everything, she thought wearily and went on up the last flight of stairs, her feet dragging.

It was deafeningly quiet in the apartment as Mia tiptoed into the hall, but while she was hanging up her outdoor clothes she heard her mother's voice coming from the bedroom.

"Is that you, Arne?"

"No, Mother, it's me. Be with you in a minute."

Mia went over to the hall mirror and looked at her flushed shiny face under the black bangs.

"I look like a ghost," she mumbled, combing through her sticky hair with her fingers and wiping her nose.

"Did I wake you up?" she said, standing in the doorway.

"Oh, no," said her mother, blinking in the light. "I hadn't gone to sleep. I sat up late with some work I'd promised I'd do for the firm, and then I went to bed and did my homework." She nodded toward the bedside table, on which lay an English grammar book.

Mia remained where she was, absorbing the warmth from the room.

The bedside lamp's orange shade spread a friendly light, which made the roses on the nylon quilt glow. There was a faint smell of the perfume in Mother's cleansing cream, and the clock on the bedhead shelf was ticking quietly and slightly irregularly as usual. This bedroom was the only room that had been really just the same after the move. It felt nice and secure to see the old beds with their scratched paintwork, the enlarged wedding photograph by the dressing table . . . the poster about bull fighting from their trip to Spain . . . Dad's ancient bathrobe on a hook by the closet . . . the cross-stitched cushion Gran had sewn in the basket chair.

Everything appeared to be "nice and secure," and Mother was lying there looking pretty in her blue nightgown, her long fair hair plaited at the back of her neck. It could have been the right moment to throw yourself into her arms and tell her everything. Mia went across and sat down on the edge of the bed.

Then she saw the wet rolled-up handkerchief on the bedside rug. Mother had been crying again.

When Mia looked up, she saw that her mother's eyelids were swollen. So it wasn't the right moment. The warmth and security of the room was an illusion. A strange mixture of impatience, disappointment, and relief came over Mia; perhaps relief more than anything else, relief over once again being able to postpone it all, scuttle back into your corner and hide, pulling the blanket over your head, pretending that if you didn't say anything, it didn't exist.

"Did you have a good time?" she heard her mother ask, but she couldn't answer. To avoid having to say anything right away, she leaned down and began to unzip her boots.

"Well, did you have a good time?" Mother repeated.

"Oh . . . sort of . . . a lot of girls from Barbro's class whom I didn't know and lots of chit-chat and sandwiches and beer and potato chips and cream cake and tea. Actually, it was kind of awful for Agneta, Barbro's sister, you know—her baby was yelling all the time."

"But—why? Isn't Agneta married, with a home of her own?"

"Yes, she was—but her husband's run off with another girl and Agneta's there alone with the kid. And since she's in her last year at nursing school, her mother has to look after the baby . . . and he's got that three-month colic or whatever it is babies get, so he just screams all day and all night. The whole family's hysterical about it. And Barbro says she's thinking of moving in with *her* boyfriend, who's got his own flat, before she goes crazy."

"So that then she can go back home with yet another baby," mumbled her mother with a grimace. "Poor things—but how can Elsa look after Agneta's child? I thought she had a job at the Post Office."

"No, she's given it up. What else could they do? They couldn't put him in a day nursery when he's sick."

"No, no, of course not." Her mother lay silent for a moment. "What a rat trap we women always end up in," she exclaimed finally, and her voice was so bitter and aggressive that Mia looked up quickly.

"But it was such a sweet baby," she heard herself say, as if she wished to defend someone.

"Babies are always sweet—that's the worst thing about it." Mia's mother laughed a little in embarrassment, as if wishing to cover up her recent sharpness of tone. "Anyway," she went on in a different tone of voice, "how are things with you? You're looking very flushed and you've black rings under your eyes. You're not sick, are you?"

"Oh, it's nothing . . . a little too much beer and running home . . . my feet were freezing. It's cold again and it's very slippery."

"Well, you really mustn't go and get sick right before Christmas. It's complicated enough already."

"Yes, it's the first of December on Saturday," sighed Mia. "They've put up the decorations in the pedestrian mall down by the shopping center already. Did you remember to buy an Advent calendar for Lillan?"

"Yes, and I even bought two, one charity one and one of the kind covered with glitter that she's been raving about—glitter all over it, with silver Christmas elves and princesses feeding squirrels and . . ."

"Oh," said Mia suddenly, smiling, "how I remember my first one—that huge one Gran gave me with a castle and hares and deer and Snow White. Golly, that seems a hundred years ago . . ."

She stopped and sat in silence. The memory of the glitter was abruptly extinguished, like snuffing out a candle.

If only it hadn't been Christmas. If only it hadn't been Christmas.

Mia's mother lay there in silence too, looking straight ahead of her. The light from the lamp suddenly seemed false, the clock malicious and irritating. Mia shivered and thrust her hands up the sleeves of her sweater.

The silence hung between them like a curtain; a transparent but impenetrable curtain, which neither of them could summon up the energy to break through.

"No, I really must go to bed now—I'm awfully tired, actually. You won't forget I can sleep late tomorrow, will you, so don't wake me until eight."

"I can't think why Arne isn't back!" Mia's mother said, glancing at the clock.

"Where is he tonight?"

"At the adult center, I think . . . or a council meeting or something . . . or auditing accounts or bowling or . . ."

Mia got up hastily. "Well, good night, then . . . sleep well."

She picked up her boots and padded over to the door.

"Same to you."

Mia had just got out into the hall when her mother called her back.

"Oh, Mia, I totally forgot. Jan called again this evening. He sounded a bit low—said he hadn't heard from you since he called last Monday."

"That's right."

"Why not, Mia? I told you it was important!"

"Oh, it's not your fault."

Her mother lay silent for a moment. "It's nothing to do with me, but is something wrong between you two?"

"I don't know."

Mia stood in the shadow just inside the door, leaning against the doorpost. She suddenly thought that she would burst from the need to talk to someone, to cry, to be comforted. Her heart raced, her mouth went dry, and she swallowed and swallowed. Hesitantly, she took a step into the room.

"You see, Mother . . ."

Just then they heard the elevator stop on the landing outside and a minute later a key was thrust into the lock.

"It's Dad at last," exclaimed Mia's mother.

Mia turned around and bolted.

"It'll be all right, you'll see," she heard her mother's encouraging voice behind her. "You can't always be on good terms."

Mia hastily closed her door and threw herself down on the bed without turning on the light. "You can't always be on good terms." Oh, God.

Through the door she heard her father's voice, shrill and irritable.

She undressed in the dark, opened the window a crack and crept into bed without either washing or brushing her teeth. She couldn't face the risk of meeting Dad in the bathroom. She couldn't even face thinking, especially about Jan. She couldn't even cry.

She lay like a stone between the cool sheets, breathing in the frosty night air that trickled in through the window.

For the first time in her life the lightning thought that it would be nice to be dead flashed through her mind.

Down there—seven floors down, the Christmas tree with its many colored lights swayed in the wind, and the clock of the concrete church squashed between Domus and the employment office tinnily struck twelve times through the clear air. It sounded like a distant music box above the sound of the traffic.

In some way, there must have been a scrap of consolation in the sound, for Mia at once fell deeply asleep, like an exhausted child.

Although she'd gone to bed so late, Mia was already awake when her mother padded out into the kitchen and put the coffee on at about seven. Otherwise, she usually slept on until someone, generally Lillan, horribly lively and cheerful, shook her awake. But things had been different lately.

Sundays and weekdays, late morning or not, she'd awaken long before she'd needed to, as if a subconscious alarm clock had gone off somewhere inside her, and before she'd even opened her eyes, her hand had automatically gone down to see if anything had happened during the night. In case her period had come.

This morning she had already long since established that nothing had happened during the night. She'd even switched on the lamp and inspected her nightgown and the sheet. Nothing.

Feeling nothing else but a kind of sleepy resignation, she crept down beneath the covers again and put out the light, lying quiet, sleep still humming in her body, struggling against that vague leaden anxiety, unable to decide what to do. And having decided, what should she do first?

It was crazy that she hadn't been to the druggist or gotten one of those things you saw advertised for doing the test yourself.

If only she could get into town. Then she could go straight to that advice bureau.

It was quite unnecessary to upset Mother if there was nothing to worry about.

And then Jan.

What was she to do about Jan? She couldn't just go on avoiding him like this.

It was crazy.

He couldn't know . . .

Anyhow, she had to find out if anything was up *before* she saw him again. She couldn't just pretend nothing was wrong.

But *if* it were a false alarm—how would he react then? Would he be angry? But it wasn't her fault, was it? He knew she couldn't use the pill. It was he who . . . who'd said it was perfectly safe. He must have lots of experience, she'd thought. He was twenty and would soon be a qualified engineer. He might have asked some time if . . . But it was at least ten days since they'd last met and then it was only . . .

She had no idea what he thought about it, about—abortion. And what did she think herself? How could she possibly think anything? She'd never given it a thought. She'd read a little about the new laws that had been proposed, of course. But not in relation to herself. *It couldn't happen to her*. But she remembered what her mother had said when she and Dad had been discussing the abortion laws.

"It's obvious that only the woman should decide whether she's going to have children or not! Isn't her life as important as that of an unborn baby's? It's only men who think they should always decide for women."

"It's not as simple as that," Dad had replied.

And another time—several years ago—her mother had said directly to her:

"Promise me something, Mia. Come to me when the time arrives and I'll help you about contraceptives; so that you don't do as I did and be forced to abandon your education and all that."

"Didn't you actually want to have me then, Mom?" Mia had asked.

Her mother had flushed a little and patted her cheek.

"Of course I want you now, darling. And to tell you the truth, I probably wanted you then, too, although there was such a fearful fuss at home. Anyway, there was no question of doing anything else in those days— You know, abortion was something unheard of then, which you weren't allowed except in very exceptional circumstances."

"But Mats, who died? Didn't you want to have him either? And Lillan? You wanted to have her, didn't you?"

"Mia darling," her mother had said, hugging her, "I wanted to have you all. All I'm trying to say is that you must be careful, so that you get a qualification before you start a family."

Mia remembered that conversation now almost word for word. But just afterward she had remembered only one thing: that her mother hadn't really wanted to have her. That had hurt. And now it was her turn. Suddenly she was a woman who had to decide whether a child, which was perhaps already inside her, should be born.

She must decide. Who else could do that? She would soon be eighteen and was strong and healthy.

Should Mother and Dad decide if she were to have an abortion? Or a school counselor? Or a doctor?

But she must want to herself. She was almost adult . . .

Lillan's shrill voice suddenly came through from the kitchen.

"Ssh! Mia's asleep."

". . . I only just lifted one corner," Lillan's voice went on, now lowered to a hiss. "I only wanted to look and see if . . . if it was just the usual baby Jesus or . . ."

"I thought it was meant to be a surprise," said her mother.

"Yes, but," cried Lillan, "it *will* be a surprise. I'll *forget* about it, don't you see . . . you know how quickly I forget things."

"Ssh! Yes, I've noticed that."

"Why's *she* sleeping late, anyway? Why can't *I* sleep late sometimes?"

Sleep late. Sleep late—pleasant soft words.

Before—that is, quite recently—ages and ages ago . . . that is, twenty-four days ago, sleeping late had been a great thing; that scrumptious half-asleep condition, when you curled up under the covers and relished the warmth of your bed and the thought of not having to get up right away and rush to the bathroom; just lying listening to the chatter of the others' voices, the clink of china, smelling the smell of coffee and cocoa blending into a sweet enticing vapor which crept through the crack in the door.

Now Mia just became anxious, lying awake in there while the others thought she was asleep, twisting and turning and needing to go to the bathroom. Today it was worse than usual since she'd gone to bed without washing or brushing her teeth. She felt sticky, her head ached, and there was a nasty taste in her mouth. If only Lillan would shut up for a second. She sounded like a noisy parrot.

The smell of coffee was suddenly unbearable. She must get up and go out. She felt as if she were going to be sick. Without putting on her robe and slippers, she darted out through the door and straight across the kitchen toward the bathroom.

"What!" cried Lillan. "Is she *awake*? And we've been sitting here as quiet as mice! What's the matter, Mia?" she cried, running after her sister. "What's all the hurry? Have you seen my advent calendar?"

"I have to go," hissed Mia, locking the bathroom door.

"Leave Mia alone, Lillan," said Mother, putting two more slices of bread into the toaster.

"No one's in such a hurry that they can't even say hello," muttered Lillan, beginning to pack her school bag. Then she brightened.

"How super that it's a nice day, isn't it? Maybe we'll be able to go skating in gym today! With our new guy."

"What new guy?"

"A kind of coach, awfully nice and awfully handsome, with his red beard! He's called Bruno . . . super name, isn't it?"

"Hurry up or you'll be late," said Dad as he came into the kitchen with the newspaper under his arm.

"Oh, Dad, it's winter outside, have you seen?"

"Your socks, Lillan. You've left your socks on the chair."

With her school bag and skates dangling around her, Lillan darted back into the kitchen, this time hopping on one leg.

"Dad, you haven't given me a kiss today," she cried, hopping over to her father, who was standing by the stove pouring himself a cup of coffee.

"For heaven's sake, stop hopping around," her mother said. "There's no time for kissing now . . . off you go."

"I'll throw one to you then—look, here it comes." Lillan waved her hand and her glove flew across the floor.

"*Lillan*!"

A moment later the front door slammed shut.

"Heavens, what vitality!"

Arne Järeberg sighed and sat down with his cup of coffee. His long face was pale, and his square glasses failed to hide the pouches under his eyes. Despite his neat checked suit and the handkerchief matching his shirt in the top pocket, and despite a fresh smell of shaving lotion, he looked tired and worried. His thin dark side hair had been carefully brushed across his bald head and the lack of hair on his head was compensated for by bushy sideburns.

"Just as well someone has some vitality," his wife said shortly, pouring out another cup. God, how I hate those sideburns, she thought. He looks like a silly old playboy.

Her husband raised his eyebrows and said nothing. He opened the newspaper and began reading as he mechanically chewed his toast, equally mechanically raising and lowering his cup of coffee.

The kitchen was just as silent now as it had been noisy and full of life a few minutes earlier; only the rustle of the newspaper, the clink of china. An artificial wounding silence lay like a strait jacket over the two people sitting at the table. Arne Järeberg chewed and rustled; his wife sat staring out through the huge picture window.

It would be another half hour before the sun rose, and all the night lights were still glittering in the retreating darkness. The sky was cloudless and soon a giant pale sun would emerge over the old school hill. They'd said on the news that it was going to be a fine sunny day with a few degrees of frost.

Arne lowered the newspaper a fraction, though not so far down that he could look his wife in the eyes.

"Aren't you going to work today?" he asked.

"I'm going to the dentist, so I've arranged for the morning off."

"Oh." The newspaper was raised again.

"Arne . . ."

"Mmm."

"Arne!"

"Yes . . ."

"Arne, put that damned paper down for a minute and look at me. I can't stand this . . ."

Then the bathroom lock clicked and Mia appeared, enveloped in her father's bathrobe. Her face shone pinkly, newly washed, and the broad eyeliner effectively hid all traces of fatigue.

"Hi!"

Mia brushed her father's lowered cheek with her lips.

"Aren't you in a hurry?"

"No, I'm free before break," mumbled Mia, going over to the stove to heat up her cocoa. "Though I forgot to tell you last night, Mother. The staff is having some conference or other. Great, isn't it? In this fine weather too."

In fact she'd decided to stay home all day. Out there in the bathroom behind the closed door, she'd decided to stay home today and think; think in peace and quiet.

No one would be back until five o'clock.

A whole long necessary day to be alone in and try to think. Making the decision alone was a relief.

"Well, I must be off now," her father said, handing over the newspaper. "I expect the car will be hard to start if it's been as cold as they say. I might not be back for supper . . . but I'll call, whatever happens."

"But you know I've got my class tonight," objected his wife, and Mia saw a quick flush spread up her face. "That's the fourth evening running you've been out."

"Can't Mia look after Lillan?"

Before either of them had time to reply, he had smiled into thin air and vanished.

Mia turned quickly to her mother, who was sitting quite still, staring at the door.

"I'd better go." Mia's mother rose slowly from her chair. She brushed her hand across her face as if she were trying to control her features. The telephone rang.

"Järeberg here. Yes. Hello, Gran.

"No, nothing much. I'm just off to the dentist. How are you?

"Oh, dear. Have you asked the nurse about it?

"Yes, that's true. It always gets worse when the weather changes.

"This evening? I'm afraid that'll be difficult. Arne said he'd probably be working overtime and I've got my class, you know. I don't dare miss that.

"Oh, yes, it's Astrid, your name day today. I'd forgotten. Oh, what a shame."

"I can go and see her this afternoon," Mia said quickly. She'd just remembered that there was a drugstore near the old people's home where her grandmother lived. "Tell her I'm coming."

"Hello, Gran, just a moment. Mia here says she'd love to come up for a while this afternoon and have some birthday cake.

"All right, we'll do that, then. She'll be along some time after four. No, of course it's no trouble. She'd love to."

"That was good of you, Mia," said her mother, putting down the receiver.

"I like going to Gran's," said Mia, getting up. It was true and yet she felt ashamed.

"Of course," said her mother hastily. "It's just that it's so hard to find the time. And all this name day business is so difficult to remember. Oh, heavens, is that the time? I must run. Don't forget to buy some flowers. Where's my bag, and I'll give you some money."

Yes, money. Money for the druggist; she'd forgotten that.

"Mother . . . there's something . . . that has to be paid in advance. You couldn't possibly give me an advance on my December money, could you?"

"Oh, so Christmas secrets are beginning already, are they?" said her mother, opening her wallet. "You've already had one advance, haven't you? It's going to be tough squaring your debts."

"I'm working in the florist's at Christmas, you know. You're supposed to get lots of tips, they say, so I'll be all right, I think. If I could have thirty kronor, that'd be fine."

"All right, that's your affair, darling."

All right, that's your affair.

Mia thought about her mother's words as she stood by the window and watched her red coat vanishing down there among the bare bushes and deserted sandpits. It was still very windy. There were a lot of cold sparrows about and the great tits were sitting like balls of feathers in the branches of the trees around the block. Mrs. Carlsson in the apartment next door was airing the bedclothes to the strains of Mozart on the radio.

All right, that's your affair.

Wonder if she would have said that if she'd known what the money was going to be used for? Never.

And whose affair was it, for that matter? That was what she had to sort out. If she'd been younger, it would have been easier in some way. Then it would have been her parents who would have had to decide. But now, she was old enough to marry even though she wasn't officially an adult. Granny, her mother's mother, had married when she was eighteen.

But if you're married . . . or if you live with someone, then you've got someone to share the responsibility. Though of course Jan had some responsibility in this too. But how many men would accept it? She'd read about the ones who just skipped out, who just said brutally to the girl that she'd have to clear up the mess herself.

Would Jan say that? No, she didn't think so. He had such kind eyes. Kind brown eyes.

But then she didn't know all that much about him.

Jan Häkansson, just twenty, a tall thin guy with kind eyes. And a beard and fairly long hair. Light brown hair and his beard a little darker. Pretty quiet . . . perhaps a bit serious, but maybe you thought that because his father was a free church minister. Jan had gone to night school and trained to be some kind of engineer, electronic or radio or something. And liked playing handball . . . going out on Saturdays or sitting in the bar, having a few beers. She'd been there with him several times. Otherwise they usually went to the movies or to Svensson's. Or just went out for a walk, sometimes just around the small open space the council had grandly named the Central Park, which her father always called Miller's Hill, because that's what it'd always been called before. Sometimes they'd taken a bus and gone out into the country and walked in the forest. Jan knew a lot about birds, which Mia did too, as Grandpa had taught her about them in Halland in the summers.

Sometimes they'd gone to a handball match, which she thought boring, although Jan got very excited.

Twice Jan had been back for a meal at Mia's and both her mother and father had said that they liked him. And she'd slept with him five times in his studio apartment in the old house behind the sports ground.

What did it mean to know a person? Well, she knew she'd fallen very much in love with him from the first moment, when they'd met in the confusion of someone's birthday party; when he'd just danced with her and walked home with her and kissed her in the doorway.

The worst thing was that now she didn't know if she knew him at all. All this worry had meant that she mostly felt a kind of . . . not exactly hostility, but . . . all her other feelings seemed to have become submerged. Sometimes she was furiously angry with him, although it was no more his fault than hers. Of course he'd persuaded her. She'd never slept with a man before.

It had seemed so safe.

It was so exhausting, all of it.

Though she had decided to go to the drugstore today, anyway. Today and not tomorrow or the day after.

Today.

That was something, anyway.

Still wearing Dad's old brown bathrobe, which smelled of White Horse and old tobacco, Mia walked around the apartment savoring her solitude. It was ages since she'd been absolutely alone at home.

The silence enveloped her in waves, filling all the corners as if it were actually a substance. The ticking of the alarm clock on the kitchen table clattered loudly through the whole apartment, making the silence even more silent.

Imagine. Having hours and hours to yourself in front of you on an ordinary weekday. Long cool hours with no rush or fuss or chat or stereo or homework or setting the table or cooking fumes or Lillan's friends pouring in, giggling and spilling fruit juice and talking about horses.

And Mother who mustn't be disturbed so that she could study.

And Dad sitting at the telephone all the time talking about regional plans and rising rents and outward-looking community activity.

Strange about this solitude, which could be so horrible, and occasionally so marvelous.

Mia went from one room to the next, taking a sandwich in the kitchen, shutting the window in the bedroom, tripping over the rocking chair's rockers, absorbing the different smells—coffee, soap, tobacco smoke, new paint.

There was still something uninhabited in the air everywhere, especially in the living room, where the furniture was new and unfriendly, too. Their old furniture had been insufficient for the new apartment.

Mother hadn't wanted to move at all. The old place had been much more rural and she'd been born in the country. But the house was to be torn down and there was nothing they could do about it.

The council had offered her father this apartment in a new high-rise close to the center and Dad had been pleased. He'd thought it was ideal to live so centrally now that he'd begun to get so many local assignments. But

Mother said that high-rises were inhuman and that the rent was too high and that they didn't really need five rooms—or four and a half, as they called it, since Mia's little room wasn't really a room.

Lillan had been just as pleased as Dad, because she would be that much nearer the riding school where she spent every spare minute. She was always talking about Alexander and Caesar and Godiva or whatever their names were, as if they were her best friends. Mia herself had been more undecided. She had been going to change schools anyway, when she'd got into high school.

Of course it was a little sad leaving your old home where you'd lived since you were born, even if it had been shabby and kind of dark. But it had only been three stories high, so everyone had known everyone else and there had been a cluster of fir trees outside where you could go sledding in the winter. Before . . . now nearly all her contemporaries had gone. So Mia hadn't really had anything against moving, although of course she'd been influenced by her mother.

Mia didn't really understand why her mother had been so against the move. Things were much better and more comfortable for her now—elevator, terrace, refrigerator and pantry and a very modern stove and lots of built-in closets and a great laundry in the basement.

And the view—from the seventh floor. It was like living on the upper deck of an Atlantic liner.

You could stand and just float out into the sunset or count thousands of stars in the evenings, stars you'd seen only in the country before. Far away the lights from the radio antenna shone like a wreath of red eyes and on the horizon the neighboring suburb lay like a glittering conglomeration of jewels. It was beautiful all right, even if there was a lot of concrete everywhere.

Mia remembered the first confused evening in the new apartment, with packing cases everywhere, bundles of bedding, wood shavings, and piles of china. There hadn't been enough light bulbs, and Lillan and she had sat in the dusk looking out through the living room's huge plate-glass windows.

It was a windy March evening, small ragged clouds flying past like little hairy gray dogs chasing each other between the rooftops. But around the square in the center the ads winked their red, green, and white lights and the unfamiliar sound of the evening commuter traffic had roared like the waves outside Granny and Grandpa's farm down in Halland.

Lillan was playing spaceship with an upside-down cake pan on her head.

"Now we're flying toward the Pole star," she shouted, pulling a number of invisible levers and pointing at a large yellow five-pointed star on top of a building soaring up on the left of their field of vision.

"Look, Mia . . . it says something. It says . . . it says . . . what does it say? I can't read what it says."

And Mia had leaned forward and spelled out the ad.

"D A T E M A," she read out slowly.

"The star's called Datema," crowed Lillan. "It sounds like Tintin."

"We live under the shadow of Datema," her mother had exclaimed when she'd seen the computer ad. "Typical!"

Neither Mia nor Lillan had really understood what she'd meant, but Mia had felt that it had been directed as a kind of reproach to her father standing beside her.

"If you think it's more human to live in the shacks with outside privies in which I grew up, then you're wrong," her father had said curtly.

"I didn't mean that."

"What *did* you mean then? You who're always finding fault with this apartment and destroying the pleasure for the rest of us."

"Now I've got to the moon," interrupted Lillan, who hadn't been listening very carefully to her parents' conversation. "And I want some food. You get awfully hungry traveling in a rocket."

But Mia had gone into the empty little room alongside the kitchen which was to be hers and had sat down on her suitcase and cried.

It was the first time she'd realized that something was happening between her mother and father, that they were becoming unhappy with each other. Perhaps it had been going on for a long time, but she hadn't understood.

That's what was so horrible about growing older.

Things weren't the way you'd thought they were.

Mia took an apple and curled up in the corner of the sofa.

Anxiety had begun to gnaw at her again and she felt an uneasy sense of nausea. It must be imagination; you don't feel sick this early, she knew that. For the umpteenth time, she took the encyclopedia out of the bookcase behind the sofa and looked up *Pregnancy.*

Pregnancy, the condition in which a woman finds herself when she is carrying within her a fertilized ovum. . . .

The normal length of pregnancy is approximately forty weeks or 280 *days or ten months of four weeks of what are known as pregnancy months. The approximate time of the end of pregnancy or beginning of delivery is usually calculated by counting from the first day of the last menstruation period one year ahead in time, then subtracting three months and adding seven days. . . .*

The ovum and the fetus within it grows extremely swiftly (see *Fetus*)*. By the end of the fourth month, the fetus is already the size of a man's head and has grown up into the abdominal cavity from the pelvis. . . .*

Mia snapped the book shut. She knew all that, didn't she? Yes, knew, knew, knew . . . that's what was so confusing.

All that you know and yet don't know.

You know lots of things but you don't understand them until you're involved yourself. Like when you're sitting looking around in the doctor's waiting room, and suddenly discovering that suffering and illness are right there beside you.

All that stuff about how a baby comes she'd known since she was five. It was a good thing to know, but not all that interesting in the long run. Then you got sex education at different stages at school and then it was quite exciting and a bit boring and some of it revolting, all that about ovaries and sperm and venereal diseases and contraceptives and that kind of thing.

It never seemed to have anything to do with yourself, really, although you understood perfectly well it was important. She'd been given a little book once, called—yes, what was it called?—*Sexual Love,* wasn't it?—but it had got lost.

You thought . . . oh, yes, I know all that—everything will work out all right. What should you do anyway? You couldn't very well go around swallowing pills for years just because some guy who wanted to sleep with you might appear on the horizon. Actually you were probably more interested in having someone to hold your hand at the movies. At least she was.

Of course there were others who were awfully advanced—at least it sounded so from all their talk. Maybe she was a little backward. But in that case, there were lots of others who were like that—girls as well as boys. Just think of Bosse, whom she'd gone around with for a while last summer—he had been overjoyed at not having to do anything.

But you had that business hanging over you all the time—that it was so necessary and natural and important and marvelously wonderful to go to bed with someone as soon as you could; that you had to feel backward or a failure or wrong in some way if you didn't; that you were awful and lousy and hopeless if you didn't want to. She hadn't really wanted to . . . but Jan . . . though she *was* in love with him. It hadn't been long before . . .

It hadn't been because she was afraid of getting pregnant. It was mostly because she'd liked things as they were. They'd got on well together without it, she'd thought.

Of course things shouldn't be as they were in the old days—lots of sanctimoniousness and sin and shame and nice girls should keep themselves pure and the others could go to hell or be ever so grateful that anyone wanted to marry them.

Of course it couldn't be wrong to go to bed with someone you're fond of.

But then you should also be able to be certain that you didn't start a baby you didn't want.

They say it's all so simple these days. Freedom and education and advice and contraceptives and almost abortion on demand and . . .

And yet.

And yet there only needs to be a little hole in a rubber sheath or some other slip-up for you to fall into the same old rat trap, as Mother had said. Then finally chaining yourself to some unwilling guy whom you'd perhaps stopped being in love with long ago, who perhaps left you at the first possible opportunity, like Agneta's husband. And they were actually married.

Or becoming a Single Parent and seeing to everything yourself and abandoning your education and trying to get a job and putting the kid into a day nursery.

Or letting your mother look after the whole thing, and perhaps letting *her* sacrifice her job and her sleep and her energy.

Equally hopeless, all of them.

If you didn't choose—abortion.

Naturally that's the only sensible thing to do if you don't want to have a child at that particular moment. But how sensible are you?

And it's horrible to read about those long lines and that women with cancer of the womb perhaps don't get treatment in time because there are so many abortion cases.

That's crazy.

But what should you do, then?

Of course, an absolutely reliable contraceptive is the only answer. Lots of girls had been frightened out of their wits by the pill for a long time, though that was in the past now, according to the papers. But if your period is irregular, they won't give you the pill. Mia had asked the school doctor herself some time last year. And the new coil hadn't really come in everywhere yet.

But even if you find the best protection in the world, then of course there are always lots of people who are just careless, or drunk, or else they don't care what happens. Or something goes wrong. Or you think nothing'll happen.

You simply can't grasp it. That a person comes into existence by sheer chance; that you can get pregnant so damned quickly. If there'd been abortion on request when Mother had got pregnant for the first time, then Mia would never have had a life to live. Quite a thought, wasn't it? Though it was horrible to think like that. She wouldn't have been harmed by not being born, and Mother would never have been able to miss her.

But Mother's life had of course become different; in what way, you didn't really know. Would she have been happier? No one would ever know. How could you know what was right? Was there any right or wrong? It was probably as Mother had said that time, that a woman must decide for herself if she wants or doesn't want to have a child at a given moment.

But of course it's easier when you're grown up and mature and know what you're doing and know that you can't afford it or can't leave your job or whatever. But—wasn't it just all those careless immature girls who really shouldn't have children? And her? She seemed to be halfway between the two.

Last night she'd dreamed about a child.

It wasn't Agneta's baby—it didn't have a face—it was just there in her arms, holding on hard to her finger with its tiny hand, smelling delicious, like rose petals.

The worst of it was that babies are always so sweet, Mother had said.

And Mia suddenly remembered Aunt Eva when she'd been visiting them and was looking at Lillan just after she was born. "Quick—take her away—she's infectious!" she'd cried. And yet Aunt Eva had four children already.

Mia knew what she meant now. She'd felt it yesterday at Barbro's house, when she'd stood there with the baby boy in her arms and he'd turned his head toward her breast and sought after her with his mouth. That longing beyond all reason.

And all that stuff you read about. The child became the love of my life and all that. Tough girls and famous actresses who stepped forward and said that children were the most wonderful thing that had ever happened to them. And poor Fabiola and poor Soraya . . .

Mia also remembered how she'd sat with some other girls in their classroom, discussing what they'd do if they'd just heard that they only had one more year to live. Lena had said at once: "I'd have a child. Not just because something of me would live after I'd died, but . . . but then I'd have used my body for something . . . absolutely . . . something important." Someone had objected that there were more important things to do for the world than give birth to one more child, but Lena had just replied: "Possibly, but that's what I feel." And nearly all the others had agreed with her.

God, what a mess.

But a person can't just be allowed to exist because all . . . just because all girls dream of being mothers. Or nearly all.

Then it would also be wrong to use contraceptives. Like it was before, when it was a sin against God to stop a person's being born. Granny had told her about an old servant they'd had when she was little who'd had lots and lots of children. When Granny's mother had said something about not having to have children every year, she had replied, "But, missus, how will I be able to stand before Our Lord at the Last Judgment? Suppose he points at a row of small souls and says, 'You should have given birth to those on earth, Alida, and you didn't.' "

She hadn't given that old story a thought for ages and ages. Now a whole lot of things were coming to the surface of her mind just to confuse her.

But even ministers approved of contraceptives nowadays, and when the whole world was overcrowded with children, there must always be someone to care for. Why wasn't there an advice bureau for this kind of thing here and not just in the very center of Stockholm?

It was a *stranger* you wanted to talk to, wasn't it? Someone outside the family, a person you had no emotional ties with or whom you needn't shame or sadden. Someone you didn't have to meet again—as you would the school counselor. Every time you met her in the hall, you'd know that she knew that that girl . . .

Mia shuddered.

No, she'd go and have a bath now, a long hot bath.

As the water was rushing into the bath, the telephone rang. It rang twice, three, four, and five times, but Mia didn't hear it.

When Mia finally staggered out of the bathroom, she was dizzy and her whole body was throbbing with heat. She threw her robe on the bed and walked around naked, her face flushed and her newly washed hair hanging in wet waves down her neck. She stood in front of the mirror to put her hair up into a roll on her head. When she'd done that, she stood there for a while, looking at her body from top to toe.

She couldn't see that it had changed—the same narrow shoulders and small breasts, the same slim waist and broad hips and too big bottom. You didn't become Miss Sweden with that figure, but that had never really worried Mia much.

She held her hands over her breasts, which felt soft and warm, almost wet after all that hot water, her nipples spread out into large circular islands. But they weren't any bigger, were they? Or tender? And her stomach? It was just as small and flat as before.

"Three weeks," she mumbled, remembering that picture of a three-week-old fetus in the encyclopedia. It had looked horrid, like a little animal with a tail, a seahorse or something.

By the end of the fourth month, the fetus is already the size of a man's head. . . .

A man's head, for heaven's sake. She cupped her hands over her navel. Then she snatched up her candy-striped nightgown, pulled it on, and stuffed a pillow over her stomach.

Oh, God, was that what you'd look like?

When she stood in profile, clasping her hands under the pillow, she looked exactly like that picture she'd seen in a magazine of the Women's Lib woman in the United States who'd said to hell with the father of the child and as a point of honor was going to be the only light in her child's life. It had sounded from the article that the child was going to have a rather rough time.

Exhaustion after the hot bath overcame her again, so she threw down the pillow and crept into her unmade bed, feeling like a large warm bun rising before baking, swelling up larger and larger.

She closed her eyes and listened to her heart, which was

still beating abnormally fast, stretched her hand tentatively out to the little transistor Jan had given her, and switched it on.

Whoever you are—welcome to the world—whoever you are—welcome to life, warbled Lill-Babs lustily out of the radio and Mia switched it off again. She hadn't the energy to listen to how Lill-Babs was urging her on to follow that unknown child on its journey and something else which rhymed with life.

Sleepily she began to leaf through an old weekly magazine which had been lying on the bedhead shelf. It was full of the Christmas joy to come:

At Advent, all the traditional preparations for Christmas begin. The days of December are carefully counted and the children usually like to have an advent calender. You can embroider one on fine natural-colored linen with small cross-stitches and mouliné wool. You line it with stiffening and edge it with red cotton tape. You can then take this advent calender out every year, so it's a good idea if the person embroidering the pretty little figures also embroiders her initials and the year at the bottom.

Pretty little tulips are planted in the same way as hyacinths and their growth time is roughly the same. When the green tip appears you carefully transplant the bulbs into white bowls and spread little stones around. . . .

Oh, God, if only it weren't Christmas.

Suddenly she hated Christmas. What stupid things. Pretty little tulips, sweet little cross-stitches, nice little surprises.

She threw down the magazine and closed her eyes

again. The clock in the concrete church struck twelve. On the last stroke, the kitchen doorbell rang. Someone was at the door.

Mia leaped out of bed so quickly that she knocked over the chair holding her clothes at the end of the bed.

Oh, I don't have to answer, she thought then, and sat down on the edge of the bed. Probably only a salesman. No one knows I'm home—except the others in the class and at this time they're all in the canteen. But all the same, she began pulling on her tights and fastening her bra.

Another long signal shrilled through the kitchen.

What a stubborn creature. But she certainly wasn't going to go out and start on about how they didn't need a new vacuum cleaner or wooden spoons or needle cases.

She snatched up her pants, dragged her turtleneck sweater over her head, and went to the mirror to do her hair, still wet after her bath and now curling a little at the ends.

Just as she'd parted it, the bell rang again, even longer this time and much more purposefully than before, the way a bell rings when the caller knows there's someone at home.

"What's going on? He must be crazy."

She lowered the comb. Suppose it's something else? Something important? Mother who'd forgotten something or Lillan who'd hurt herself at school? She stood there listening. Suppose it was a thief ringing for a long time to ensure that no one was at home?

If only they had a peephole in the door.

A fourth ring made her jump. Then a loud knocking. Someone outside shouted something she couldn't hear.

Afterward, she couldn't imagine why she hadn't realized right away that it was Jan.

She was so shocked that she remained standing absolutely immobile, her hand still on the doorhandle. Without a word.

She didn't want to see him now. Not now when she didn't know. Not now when she couldn't tell him why she'd been avoiding him.

"Oh, it's you," she managed to say at last.

"Yes, it is. Can I come in? Are you alone?"

"Of course, come in," she mumbled mechanically. There was nothing else to say. "Yes, well, I'm alone, had . . . had such a headache this morning . . . so . . . so Mother thought I'd better stay home."

"Is it better now?" He hung up his sheepskin jacket.

"What?" Mia was still standing with her back to the door, avoiding looking at him, her thoughts whirling around in her head in helpless indecision. God, what was she going to say?

"I asked you if your headache had gone away."

"Yes, thanks, yes, it has." She fell silent again. "Won't you come in . . . would you like some coffee or something? Actually, I haven't had any lunch yet."

That would be O.K. Then she'd have a little time to think things out. She had to explain.

Mia let him go ahead into the kitchen. He was just as confused as she was. She saw him standing in the middle of the kitchen floor against the light from the big window, rocking on his heels, running his hand in embarrassment over his beard and hair, breathing on his hands, which were red and cold.

She hadn't seen him for ten days. She'd forgotten what he looked like.

She stood there with the coffee pot in her hand, taking him in at a glance, and suddenly like a wave it all welled up in her. . . . Oh, God, how could I have thought it'd be any different?

If Jan had looked at her then, in the next second she'd have been in his arms, forgetting everything else except the emotion that rushed through her.

But Jan had turned around and walked over to the window.

Mia stood there with her coffee pot, staring at his back, not knowing what she should do with all the wild marvelousness singing inside her, trying to get out. She took a step forward.

"Why didn't you call, Mia?" He didn't turn around, but was speaking at the windowpane, his tone aggressive. "I've phoned you three times."

It was as if she'd been punched in the stomach, a sharp blow that forced her to return to reality again, a blow which suddenly made her see that her feelings for Jan were really of no significance at this moment.

Mechanically, Mia filled the coffee pot with water and put it on the stove, went over to the refrigerator and took out eggs and butter, milk and cheese and a package of smoked sausage, her arms and legs functioning entirely independently.

She blinked and fumbled blindly for the breadknife. It

was terribly important not to . . . it was so horribly tempting.

Mia was silent. God in heaven, what should she do? Tell a lie and say she wasn't in love with him any more, that she had met someone else, and that was why she hadn't called? That was an awful way to treat him, but if she didn't think of anything else, she'd have to tell him the truth.

"Aren't you listening to what I'm saying, for Christ's sake? What have I done wrong for you to behave like this?"

"Come and eat now," Mia said hastily. "Then we can talk about it afterward. I'm awfully hungry."

But of course it didn't work, sitting there, eating eggs and sausage and pretending nothing was up.

In the middle of her egg, Mia burst into tears.

She was overwhelmed so rapidly that she hadn't expected it the second before it happened; something just snapped and it all poured out.

Jan, who'd been sitting sulkily on the other side of the table, chewing on crispbread and cheese so loudly that it echoed in the silence, leaped to his feet.

"Mia . . . darling . . . what's the matter?"

But Mia just wept and wept, all the tears she'd wanted to weep all these last days and weeks; all her uncertainty and anguish became a violent flood of tears which poured down on to her egg and bread.

"Come!" Jan dragged her away from the table and into her room and then sat her carefully down on her bed, but as soon as he let go of her, she threw herself down into the bedclothes and went on crying. Finally her tears became a hysterical wailing, which she tried to muffle in the quilt.

"Mia, calm down. What's happened? Look, have a drink of water." He sat down beside her on the bed and tried to raise her head. But she pushed both him and the glass away.

In the end, he just sat there and waited with his head in his hands. He heard her sobs gradually subsiding.

"Mia," he said. "Whatever it is, can't you talk about it?"

Whatever it is! *Whatever it is.* Could it be anything else but one thing? Did he really have no idea? A peculiar rage overcame her despair. She sat up with a jerk and stretched out for a piece of sheet to blow her nose. She didn't look at him, just felt his hand on her thigh.

"I think I'm pregnant," she said suddenly, calmly, but her voice was thick.

The silence that followed seemed to Mia to last for hours, forever. It grew so long that she felt she'd had time to think hundreds of yards of thoughts. It grew so long that she felt that . . . yes, literally felt, in fact . . . that she'd had time to become adult. So adult that she could think: I wonder how many million million stunned young men have sat like this and just said nothing? And thought feverishly.

"Are you sure?" he said finally.

"No, not really."

"How long?"

"Over three weeks."

"Have you had a test?"

"I'm going today."

"But why didn't you go before? You can tell after eleven days."

"Oh, you know that, do you?"

"For God's sake, Mia, if it's not true it's crazy to go around worrying."

"Condoms aren't all that safe, as you said."

"Nothing's really safe, you know that."

Mia was thinking all the time that this must be some unknown girl—someone outside herself—talking and answering, like being at the theater. They made exactly the remarks that are always made in this situation: impersonally automatic.

"Come on," she said suddenly. "Come on into the living room, and we'll have some coffee, then we can talk about this properly."

She went in a few minutes later, washed and tidy and with the tray in her hands. Jan was sitting in an armchair, smoking a cigarette.

His thin boyish face was gloomy and he didn't look up when Mia came in. He looks like a little boy at the dentist's, she thought, and suddenly she felt a great tenderness for him. She knew that he cared for her—otherwise he wouldn't have made such a fuss about her not calling him. She also knew now that she cared about him too, a lot, and she wouldn't really mind having a child by him at all. If only things were as easy as that.

The simplest thing would have been to go up to him and throw her arms around his neck. Instead she put the tray down on the low table and sat herself down on the sofa, a long way away from him.

"You don't take cream, do you?"

"Mia . . ."

"Yes?"

"I suppose it's not worth discussing anything until we know for certain."

"That's exactly why I didn't want to see you. I didn't want to worry you unnecessarily. On the other hand, now you do know, it's perhaps best that we talk about it. We have to—in case it *is* so, and then we have to decide, don't we?"

Jan sat in silence, stirring his coffee to occupy his hands.

"It's come at a hell of an awkward time," he said finally. "Just now."

"What do you mean 'awkward'? These things always come at awkward times."

"I mean . . . before I've got a job and all that . . . and in these difficult times."

"What do you mean? You don't have to marry me, if that's what you think."

"Move in together, then—it's the same thing, isn't it? —though Dad would . . ."

"I'm not thinking of moving in with you."

Strange, thought Mia, it's going on, this feeling of unreality. Suddenly I'm saying things I didn't know I'd thought of saying, as if decisions had been made by themselves in my head, without my being conscious of it.

The next instant she felt Jan's arms around her and his hand on her chin.

"Look at me, Mia. What's wrong with you? Why do you sound like a robot? Don't you care for me any longer?"

"Yes," said Mia gently. "I've just realized I love you."

She put her head against his shoulder and thrust her

hand into his. For a moment they sat still, simply feeling the warmth of each other's bodies. "But there is *one* thing."

"What? Isn't that the most important thing?"

"Well, sure it's great that we like each other, but it doesn't solve the problem of the child just like that—if it is so. Not as I see it, anyway. I'm not leaving school and all my education to stay at home to look after children."

"But . . ."

"Hush a minute and let me finish. You don't want a family just yet either, in fact, or to get yourself a whole lot of debts now before you even know if you can get a job. It'd be crazy. We'd be there in your one-room apartment with a yelling baby, living on welfare. We'd be hating each other in six months."

"Maybe your mother would . . ."

"My mother cannot possibly . . . she's got enough on her own plate."

"Yes, my mother's got a job too, like yours."

"You can't count on mothers today—haven't you found that out? This is our affair and ours alone."

"But then there's no other solution except to get married . . . to live together?"

"Yes, there is. If the results are positive, then I'm thinking of asking for an—abortion."

Jan took his arm away from Mia's shoulders and sat and said nothing for a long time.

Mia could hear him swallowing repeatedly. Then he got up and began walking around the room.

"That's against everything I've ever been taught at home," he said finally.

"What?"

"That abortion is murder and you can only resort to it in certain definite circumstances. I can't possibly contemplate the idea."

"It's my affair."

"It's my child, too, for Christ's sake."

"You mean then that you're willing to wreck my whole future and your finances and everything else because your parents consider that—that it's wrong. You don't even believe in God, as far as I know."

He was silent. She went on:

"Of course, *I* don't think it's much fun *either*, I'll have you know, and abortion isn't something people can resort to the minute some contraceptive doesn't work or whatever . . . but it is *one* thing."

"But Mia . . . there are lots of people our age who have children and they manage. There are lots of so-called unwanted children who get on fine and are loved and . . ."

"But there are also lots of unwanted children who've landed up in children's homes or with lonely unhappy mothers who've worked themselves to death and who've become criminals and gone right downhill."

"But that wouldn't happen to our child."

"How do you *know*? And even if it *didn't* land up in a children's home or become a criminal, suppose we begin to fight and separate and . . . or I sit at home getting bitter because I couldn't be what I'd wanted to be and quarrel and nag . . ."

Jan gestured violently with his arm.

"You exaggerate too much. For God's sake. Mia! I just can't talk any sense with you. Let's stop this here and now.

It's only a . . . a theoretical discussion anyway. If it's a false alarm."

"Yes, but we must know what we *think,* Jan. Don't you see? We must take up a position . . . know what we want, in case."

"Well, you know now . . . what I think."

"You mean, then, that if I'm willing to give birth to this possible child because of your views on abortion, then you're willing to look after this possible child and share jobs and give up handball and lots of other things to stay at home with the baby while I study or get a training in some other way. *Are you?*"

"It's silly to put the whole thing like that, when we don't even know if it is anything."

"But it might happen *again,* Jan. It might happen again. All right, all right, don't let's talk about it any more, if you don't want to. I know what you think now, and of course it's important to listen to different views on things like this. But even if you say it's unnecessary to discuss it purely theoretically, I think it's important that we know where we stand with each other."

"But Mia . . ." Jan turned toward her and his voice was suddenly gentle. Mia saw with astonishment that his mouth was trembling. "Mia, are you yourself sure that . . . that you want to . . . sure that it's right—for us?"

She didn't reply at first. Then she threw herself down on the sofa and buried her head in a cushion. Jan could see that her shoulders were shaking, and in two strides he was beside her.

"But Mia, darling."

"Of course I'm not sure," she sobbed. "How could I be? But who, tell me . . . *who* can decide that for you? How can you ever say that it was better that *this* happened than *that,* when you can't know anything about life in advance. If you think like this . . . if I take this one away, then perhaps I'll never have any more children . . . then later when I want them myself— That's happened before. Of course, then you blame yourself. But you can't always say that. If if if—forever and ever."

"Anyway we don't have to decide anything at this very minute," mumbled Jan, his face against her breast. She drew her hand through the thick hair at the back of his neck and for a second all her problems disappeared and the only really important thing was to hold him close to her. She rubbed her wet eyes against his sleeve and turned up her mouth to be kissed.

"Mia," he mumbled after a while. "Mia, come on, let's go into your room . . . if we've had it already, then . . ."

"You're crazy!" She sat up with a jerk. "You really are crazy. I think I'm going insane."

"I'm already insane," he muttered, burying his head in her throat.

"Jan. Listen, Jan! Get up. I've got to go see Gran and eat birthday cake."

"What did you say?"

"Eat birthday cake, I said."

"*You're* crazy."

Mia sat in a window seat at the back of the bus, as unconscious of her surroundings as if she'd been sitting alone on a stone in the forest. She seemed to be floating freely around her confused and contradictory thoughts, seeing and hearing, and yet blind and deaf.

She stared at the fat black headlines on the posters outside the cigar store where the bus had stopped, but afterward she didn't know what they had said.

Mechanically she read POLITICAL ASYLUM FOR CHENG scrawled on the library wall, but she couldn't remember who Cheng was or when it had happened. It could have been six months or a month ago. In Domus's store windows there was that fur-trimmed jacket that she'd dreamed of as a Christmas present only a few weeks ago. Now she didn't even look in that direction.

Half a class of kids stormed onto the bus at the stop below the new Högbergs School, but she didn't notice the confusion and noise. Although the setting sun was shining straight into her eyes as the bus swung out to the open field by the sea, she just turned her head away, ignoring the turquoise sky above the frosty reeded edge of the sea, where the ducks lay stiffly, taken by surprise by the cold; she didn't even notice the fresh winter air that swept into the bus's fusty warmth every time the door was opened to let passengers on. Mia was sitting in her own private little shelter, noticing nothing.

It was a miracle that she'd actually remembered to take the bottle with her urine sample in it, which she'd fixed that morning and hidden in the medicine chest. But the flowers for her grandmother she had, of course, forgotten.

"Listen, let's get married," Jan had said suddenly in the elevator, kissing her so hard she could hardly breathe.

"You're crazy."

"You can't stay at school all through the spring term and be pregnant, can you?"

"But what will I do then?"

"Well, you could stay at home in my kitchenette and cook my meals for me when I get back from work . . . or knit those small things that they have to have."

"But what if you don't get a job?"

"Oh, things'll work out."

That was when the bus came.

Everything had become even more confused than before. How much simpler it would have been in some ways if he'd said: "You have to get rid of it." As most of them say. And then she'd have been angry and said: "I'll do as I like."

But he'd been so nice. And she loved him.

But she didn't want to get married. Or leave school. Or cook meals. Before she was eighteen.

It was crazy. Mother would have a fit.

Anyway, Jan probably didn't want to get married either, when it came to the crunch. That was probably purely *theoretical* too.

The woman at the drugstore looked impersonally friendly as she received Mia's clumsily wrapped-up bottle.

"It's for . . . for a . . . pre . . . pregnancy test," she mumbled, hating herself for sounding so silly.

But the friendly white coat was used to this.

"Oh, yes," she said, taking out a printed card.

"Do you want . . . my name and address?" Mia's voice sounded a little more confident now.

"Oh, no, that's not necessary, but your identification number, please, and the date of your last period."

Mia looked swiftly around before whispering her answers. It was stupid—no one knew her here, but that's what happened all the same, as if she needed to feel ashamed before the woman.

"That's it, then. You can come for it tomorrow."

"Tomorrow? I thought you could get it the same day."

"Then you have to bring the sample in before two o'clock, I'm afraid," she said imperturbably.

"But—I don't live around here at all . . . and . . . I don't think I can come here tomorrow. Can I call for the result?"

"Yes," said the woman. "Usually we like it to be picked up here, but of course in an emergency it's all right to phone."

"Oh, that'd be awfully good of you . . . you see . . ."

She stopped and began to fumble in her bag.

"How much is it?"

"Twenty kronor fifty-five, please."

"Twenty, fifty-five?"

"Yes, tax included."

It was a little cheaper than she'd thought. Someone had said it was twenty-five, but maybe it was different at different places.

One krona fifty to the good, she thought, as she left the bright warmth of the drugstore and stepped out into the small asphalt square that constituted the shopping center of Gran's part of the suburb, the square with its Co-op and Fish-and-Fruit and the cigar store and the sickness benefit office and the local branch of the bank. And the old people's home farthest away, like a brick rectangle glittering with windows, a little garden around it and two forgotten pine trees at one corner.

Mia walked around the square twice.

She needed to calm down for a while before she went up to her grandmother. The tension of the bus ride had given way a little, now that the job was done, but she needed some fresh air in her lungs and some distraction to her thoughts so that Gran's eyes didn't see straight through her.

It was so strange with Gran these days, fine in a way. Before, Mia had always been a little afraid of her, she had seemed so silent and stern, at least in comparison with Granny, her mother's mother. When Mia was small, she'd always preferred Granny, who was soft and frizzy and very talkative and much younger than Gran.

But now it was almost the other way around. You could

talk easily with Gran, and she read so many books, devouring nearly everything the librarian brought her. Gran used to say that she had acquired a taste for the printed word from the time when she had delivered newspapers in the early mornings, an excellent job for someone with a lot of children, she said, because then you came home when the children had woken up. But think of getting up at three o'clock every morning and going off on a bicycle with heavy packs of newspapers in all kinds of weather. No wonder she seemed so crippled with arthritis and tired.

The sad thing was that they so seldom had time to visit her. Mother said that Gran was constantly on her conscience, which always sounded so grim. It couldn't be much fun being on someone else's conscience. But it was the same with Mia, and although she liked seeing Gran, weeks would go by, or even longer, between Mia's visits.

No one had time. Everybody was always rushing around. Mother had her job and her evening classes, Dad had his job and all his council duties, Mia her school and homework and friends, and Lillan her school and her horses. It was almost the same for all of them. And people talked about improving the environment and a more natural society and all that, but no one had time for others.

It was crazy.

But Gran used to say that in the old days when people had plenty of time, they were no happier for that, because there was so much else they didn't have.

Mia bought five pink carnations for Gran at the Fish-and-Fruit. With her mother's money. And a small bunch of grapes from herself with the leftover money. That was a good use to put it to, though she wondered what Gran would say if Mia told her that the grapes had been bought with money left over from a pregnancy test.

She probably wouldn't be shocked. Mia had noticed that she was often more tolerant than lots of younger people. "You become indulgent when you get old," Gran had said once. "I don't know whether it's out of laziness or wisdom."

And yet Mia didn't think she wanted to talk to Gran about it at all. What could she do? She'd just worry and sleep even worse at night.

Gran was wearing the bright blue corduroy dress that Mia loved. All the other old women were always so flowery, and the blue corduroy brought out the blue in Gran's eyes and the pink in her cheeks.

Mia was also glad that Gran had smooth hair with straight bangs instead of small curls all over her head, and that she smelled so good of the Cologne Dad always gave her for Christmas. "Old women should smell nice," she used to say.

"It is nice of you to come, Mia dear," said Gran, holding out her swollen, deformed hand. "And flowers and grapes, too. Well, thank you, dear, and only a name day. Well, perhaps you think it's silly to celebrate name days," she went on, "but the old things here are like leeches the way they go on and on about it. 'Well, is anyone coming for your Astrid day this year, my dear? Astrid Persson is expecting her *whole* family and Astrid Lungberg has been invited to her son's place in Västeras. . . .' Until you get tired of it all and call up and remind the family. It's a pity Arne is the only one of my children who lives in town. . . . Well, I say in town, though it's only a suburb. Otherwise he could have been relieved of the burden of name days and all the nonsenses grandmothers think up."

"It suited me very well to come today, actually," said Mia, feeling somewhat ashamed inside. "And I'm dying for some cream cake."

"It's in the refrigerator out there in the pantry—and there's coffee in the Thermos on the table. Or a soda—which would you prefer?"

"Oh, a soda, please, Gran."

Gran had lit candles on the table and had got out her best embroidered tablecloth. All the furniture except the bed was her own and the room was cozy, though small. Above her armchair hung a portrait of Grandad in his railroad uniform.

"You're almost grown up, my dear," Gran said suddenly, bending forward.

Mia flushed. "What do you mean? Grown up!" She laughed. "I haven't grown since I was here last month."

"No, but something in the expression on your face," said Gran. "Something different and . . . and maturer. You're in love, I suppose."

"Maybe."

"And you've grown very like your father . . . same narrow face and same coloring. Though"—she went on with a sigh—"he hasn't much color left at all, poor thing. He just looked gray and exhausted when he was here last."

"He's got too much to do. He's almost never at home in the evening."

Gran sat silent, stirring her coffee. "I don't think he likes his job."

"He doesn't? He never says anything about it. But he got better pay after the amalgamation."

"Pay," snorted Gran, swallowing the last gulp of coffee. "Pay . . . your pay doesn't mean everything, though people seem to think so nowadays. It's independence and responsibility that count, you know. As I expect you realize, he feels he's only an insignificant little cog in that huge company. At Anderssons Metal Company he had a say, but now he's got lots of people above him deciding . . . and that's no fun when you're nearly fifty. That's why he looks so gray. It gnaws at him from the inside, I can see it. He can't bear that, Arne can't. He's always been concerned about his self-esteem."

"But he's got a lot of say on committees and in his volunteer groups," protested Mia.

"Yes, yes, it's a good thing he can feel he has some influence somewhere, but I think he'll make a hash of himself in the end."

Mia sat saying nothing, crunching a cocktail cracker.

She'd never thought that that was what was behind it. Dad had just said that he was better paid with the new firm, except, now that she thought about it, it was last year and just about the time of the amalgamation that he'd begun to look so tired and miserable. And never came home in the evenings. . . .

"And your mother?" Gran asked, emptying the bottle into Mia's glass. "How are her studies going?"

"Very well, I think, thanks. She'll finish English by Christmas and then she's going to start on math."

"How clever she is—a job and studying and running the home. And I'm sure she doesn't get much help from Arne. We didn't have the sense to bring up boys to help in our day, I'm afraid."

"But Dad has his own things to do," said Mia defensively.

"Yes, I know . . . but it's not surprising that there are so few women in politics, is it? They simply can't manage everything."

Mia said nothing. She didn't like Gran's speaking ill of Dad.

"Anyway, I think that deep down inside Arne doesn't really like your mother's working in a store or studying," Gran said after a while.

"Why do you think that? I've never noticed it. He must be very pleased she can earn some money. And when she's qualified and gets a better job, then she can earn more. He must think that's a good thing."

"Some men like to be the only one earning."

"But that was in the old days, Gran, not nowadays."

"I'm afraid your father is a typically old-fashioned man in that respect, Mia dear." She sat in silence for a while, fidgeting with the chain on her glasses.

"I don't think it's easy to be the middle generation today . . . like Arne. They grew up with unemployment and crises in the thirties and then the war came and the draft. And then finally the good times that everyone had dreamed about for so long came along. And all the reforms. And all the things you could get. And lots of work opportunities—you could just choose. And you thought it'd never come to an end. We went and became middle class, all of us," she said, turning her head and gazing absently out of the window.

Mia didn't really know what to say. Gran was twisting and turning the chain in her fingers and you could see her thoughts were wandering.

"I think it was silly that they ever married," she said finally, looking at Mia as if she couldn't remember who she was talking to, as if she had completed a thought process she'd been turning over in her mind for a long time.

"It was a wicked shame that that girl couldn't go on with her education," she went on, as if to herself. "But what else could you do in those days except stay at home with the child? I couldn't help her, with my wretched hands—and her mother lived so far away. And Arne was a grown man—nearly thirty . . . he wanted to get married."

"Mother told me that she wanted to get married too . . . that they were desperately in love," Mia burst out. It was horrible, talking like this about what until quite recently had been the most obvious and safe thing in life.

"Yes, forgive me, Mia dear. . . ." Gran suddenly pulled herself together. "Of course they were in love . . . but Marianne was so young and I get so angry when I think of how slow it all is with what they call liberation for us women. Thank God it is at least getting better now for the younger generation . . . day-care centers and maternity benefits and all that. Though I don't like all this running down of men as if they were natural enemies, even if Arne makes me angry sometimes. But it's not his fault. It's mine and society's and the development of the century and ideas. It won't do us any good to run men down now, because that's what they did with us before. The only thing to do is to get a career and money of your own . . . without money, we'll never get equality, believe you me."

"Mmm," mumbled Mia, wondering what her grandmother would have thought if she'd heard what Jan had said about Mia staying in his kitchenette and cooking his meals.

"Anyway, Mia dear, we haven't said anything about you. You started in high school this fall—yes, you told me that, but I don't remember what subjects you're taking or what your plans are for the future."

"I'm on the science side, actually . . . you don't need such awfully high marks to get in now and I'm thinking of being . . . some kind of chemist one day, if I can keep up. Chemistry's always been my best subject—but you never know."

"You never know," said Gran, and Mia suddenly felt her old fear of her sternness. "Never know—it's only a matter of working hard and sticking to it."

"Maybe it's not as simple as that," mumbled Mia.

"No, whoever said things should be simple? Life is never especially simple, whatever times one lives in, I'll have you know. It's this so-called welfare state that's made people think that everything should just land in their laps."

"But the welfare state has been a good thing—just look at this home and how fine and comfortable it is compared with the old one down by the police station, where Grandad lived."

"Oh, yes, I know it's fine." Gran put her glasses on as if wishing to register its advantages.

"It's excellent. We have everything we could wish for . . . good beds, good food, hairdressers and chiropodists and therapy and advice, physical fitness, and bingo. And marvelous baths for invalids . . . Sunday services and books and television. And a kind superintendent and nice girls who wash our backsides and push our wheelchairs and . . ."

She fell silent and once again Mia felt that Gran wasn't talking to her, but to herself.

"And yet . . . and yet the only thing we really long for is someone who'd have time to talk to us sensibly . . . that we mean something to an individual person." She ran her hand over her eyes. "That . . . that it really matters a little that we are actually *alive*."

"I see, but . . ."

"No, my dear, you *don't* see. You never understand anything in life until you're actually involved in it, you know. And you mustn't take that as a kind of reproach—promise me that, because I didn't mean it that way. But it's so good to be able to talk to one's own sometimes—a young person who isn't stuck yet into the wretched everyday routine. Sometimes I get so deathly sick of hearing about all the Christmas runners and knitted cardigans and other people's grandchildren and their little ways and the Reverend Hammarberg's excellent qualities that I could scream."

"But—I thought—that . . . that you liked it here, Gran."

"But, my dear child, of course I like it here and couldn't have things better anywhere else. Don't think I want to come and live with you. . . . I simply couldn't cope with that. Only healthy young people come up with all those well-meaning ideas about how the old can look after small children and all that. No, heaven preserve us . . . no . . . I like it here all right.

"You see, it's just that sometimes I don't really like this exhausting life. People rush around for a while and struggle and strive and get power in different directions. And some things get better, and a lot of things have indeed gotten better—but some things get worse, and some people believe that God should change people's hearts and others believe that revolution would do it. And evil is there all the time and sometimes it blossoms forth in full bloom like with Hitler and in Vietnam and . . .

"No, no, Mia dear—I'm beginning to sound like an evangelical preacher at a prayer meeting. Finish up the last bit of cake, will you—it'll only go sour and my old stomach won't stand any more. And tell me what you all want for Christmas. I hope Lillan will send me a list as she usually does. I must have a lot of notice. It's always difficult to get these things done for you. The girls here have enough to do already."

"I could help you shop, if you like."

"Thank you, dear, I won't say no to that offer . . . I'll keep you to that. Thank you very much. Well, just think, Christmas again already. I used to think Christmas was such fun, with all the fuss and things to do—but now it's all so forced."

"But you're coming to us as usual, aren't you, Gran?"

"Oh, yes, please, I hope so, as long as I'm well enough."

Going home on the bus, Mia sat in the same place at the back as she'd had before, and now as then, she was absorbed in her thoughts. But now she wasn't thinking about herself.

She was thinking about Gran and what she had said. About Mother and Dad and all the rest of it. It was as if someone had drawn aside a veil.

Poor everyone. Poor Dad. She was thinking most about him.

Before, when she was small, Mia had really always been more Dad's girl than her mother's. Dad had looked after her a lot when Mother had had Mats, who'd died when he was two months old, and Mother was unwell for so long. And then when Lillan was born . . .

But later on it was the other way around. When Mia was in her teens, she and her mother had had more in common and Lillan had seemed to take over Dad. He read her stories at night, taught her on Sundays to ride a bicycle and skate. Mia seemed to lose him and had never really thought about what it was like for him. Sometimes she'd noticed that he didn't seem so happy as before, but she soon forgot that. Lately she'd mostly felt critical toward him because he seemed to be avoiding them all and leaving Mother on her own.

When Mia walked into the hall, her mother was standing there with her coat on.

"Heavens, you're late. How was Gran? You didn't forget to buy her some flowers, did you? Your supper's in the oven—I've got to go now . . ."

And Lillan came out and shouted, "Come and look, Mia, they're repeating *Follyfoot.*"

Oh, help, thought Mia. I'm so flat out I think I'm going to be sick.

The public telephone at school was out of order when Mia went to phone the drugstore the next day. It took her two breaks to discover the fact. When she rushed down in the third break to the cigar store across the street, the telephone was occupied by someone who had forgotten her key and couldn't get back home. Mia waited for as long as possible but in the end had to run back.

They were having an oral test in chemistry.

"Some people seem to have their heads tucked under their arms today," said her chemistry teacher genially, when Mia answered incorrectly for the third time.

If only you knew, you silly old fool, you, Mia thought, sticking her nose in the air, so that no one would notice how close she'd been to bawling her head off.

Jan was to meet her outside school at a quarter to four. He thought she'd know by then.

God, she felt sick. Her head ached like mad. The air in the classroom was close and stuffy and the smell from the things on the table was revolting.

Bengt and Svante were sitting behind her whispering about a girl they'd met at the discotheque.

Lotta was writing formulas on the blackboard, the chalk screeching agonizingly, her sweater turning white with dust. Her voice intoned monotonously:

". . . as with silver salts, the hydrogen halides shows similar molecular structures. They are colorless acid gases and very soluble in water. Sulfuric acid is used in their preparation."

"She must have just come to town," whispered Svante.

If the bell doesn't ring soon, I'll die, thought Mia.

"Fluorides do not give precipitates with Tollen's solution; AgF is not as difficult to dissolve as the others are . . ." Lotta droned on.

"She seems fine to me," hissed Bengt.

Oh, God, don't let me faint, or everyone will think I'm pregnant.

"Aren't you feeling well, Mia?" she heard the teacher's voice penetrating through the roar. "You may go out if you're feeling unwell."

How she got out, she didn't know. But she heard the whispers.

"She looks green . . . ."

"It's her period. I'm like that sometimes."

Lena, the monitor, went out with her and gave her a drink of water.

"Do you want an aspirin?"

Mia shook her head.

"But that usually works when you've got a pain in your stomach."

"Thanks, but I think it'd be best if I got out into the fresh air."

"Do you want me to go home with you?"

"No, thanks. Jan's meeting me."

"Oh, I see, then . . ."

There wasn't much of the lesson left and when Mia went out through the school entrance, Jan was already standing by the corner store, smoking a cigarette.

"Hi," he said, his face expressionless.

"Hi," said Mia and started walking down the street.

"So it's happened," said Jan, as they swung into the lane down to the riding school.

"Why do you think that?"

"You look awful."

"I felt sick in chemistry and had to go out."

"But the drugstore then? What did they say at the *drugstore* when—Mia!" He swung her around.

"I don't *know* . . . I mean, I didn't get the results yet. It was too late yesterday—I should have gotten there before two. I was to call today, but I couldn't get hold of a telephone."

"Don't be crazy. There are *thousands* of phones."

"What's the matter with you—do you think I haven't *tried*? I'm just as nervous as you are, for God's sake."

"Then let's go back to my place and call. It's not far. Then we can have some tea or something. Mia, don't look so awful."

"I feel awful."

At first Mia didn't hear what the person at the other end of the phone said. Her hand on the receiver was trembling so much that she had to hold on to it with her other hand. Her palms were wet and sticky and she could feel her hair sticking to her forehead with sweat, although it was cold in the room. Jan had gone out to the kitchenette and was clattering around with cups.

"What?" repeated Mia. "Has to be . . . *has to be done again*. Why?"

The clear impersonal voice in the receiver explained.

"So you're not *certain*? So I have to . . . come . . . another sample. When will I get the results from that, then? On Monday. Not until Monday!" Mia almost screamed.

"Yes, yes, I'll come then . . . what? Morning sample—preferably."

Jan was standing beside her with the breadknife in his hand as she hung up.

"Is something wrong? Didn't they tell you?"

"No, it wasn't certain. They couldn't say for certain," she said, her voice thick. "And so I have to give them another sample. Tomorrow morning. I think I'll go *mad*!" Mia threw herself down on to Jan's sofabed and burst into tears. "And since it's Saturday tomorrow . . . then . . . then I can't get it until—Monday. Until Monday—it's insane. I simply can't *stand* it."

"But if it's uncertain, then perhaps it's nothing," said Jan. "That's *better* than if they'd said it was positive, anyway, isn't it? Listen, Mia—admit that!"

"Anything's better than not knowing," sobbed Mia.

"Here, have some tea and I'll go out and do a bit of shopping, then you can lie here and sleep for a while. Make yourself a sandwich."

"But it's my turn to cook dinner at home—it's Friday and Mother's doing overtime at the store."

"Your father, then? He could do the dinner—he finishes work at five o'clock. Call him at the office and tell him you've been held up."

"Held up! That sounds crazy. I must find a real excuse."

"Tell him you've been invited out to dinner, then, for God's sake. You've got a life of your own, haven't you?"

"But suppose he's got an important meeting to go to."

"Then he can damned well skip it for once!"

"He'll have a fit."

"Let him."

"You're kind, Jan," whispered Mia, rubbing her nose against his beard.

Mia woke at the sound of Jan's key in the front door. Had she slept that long? She hadn't meant to sleep, only rest for a while, creeping in under the coverlet and turning out the light on the bedside table because it hurt her eyes. And then she'd just passed out.

She stretched and blinked toward the window. A Christmas garland of multicolored lights above the bakery on the other side of the street hung in the lower part of the window. Feet pattered on the sidewalk below and someone was racing a car engine.

It was cool and pleasant in the room and her headache had vanished. She heard Jan creeping about out in the hall, rustling paper bags.

"Hi!" she called. He came in at once and switched on the overhead light.

"Did you sleep well?" he asked. His cheeks were red with cold, and when he bent over to kiss her his beard was damp and smelled good, of winter.

"Boy, I'm hungry," Mia said suddenly, pushing him away. "I'm starving."

"I bought T-bone steak," said Jan.

"That's great."

"And cheese and French bread and grapes and two vanilla cakes to have with coffee."

"Jan, you're crazy," she cried, throwing her arms around his neck and sitting for a long spell with her face against his throat, without moving or saying anything. In the apartment above someone was tinkling *My Fair Lady* on a piano. "Listen, Jan. Let's forget everything for this evening. We'll pretend it doesn't exist . . . just have a good time and have a meal and light a fire. It's ages and ages since I last had a nice evening. In fact, it seems like a hundred years. And Jan—don't let's make love tonight—I couldn't cope. Let's just sit here, close to each other, holding on to one another—Jan—what do you think?"

"Of course," said Jan, kissing her nose. "I'll peel the potatoes and you can fry the steak."

Four hours later, as Mia was going up in the elevator at home with her mouth still soft and damp from Jan's parting kisses, she felt strangely exhilarated. All her anxiety for the future had been encapsulated, as if in a chrysalis deep down inside her. It had been a wonderful evening.

They had eaten well and drunk a little wine, not so much that they had got excited, but enough to help them forget the coming Monday. They'd sat on Jan's broken-down old sofa which he'd bought from the Salvation Army and listened to his Gilbert O'Sullivan record and stared at the glowing fire and told each other about their childhood Christmases and wonderful summers, when they'd built cabins and made toffee on a fire on the rocks. And Jan had been serious and told her how difficult it was for him now, when he didn't believe in God, to go through the whole Christmas ritual at home with his parents and going to church and all that.

"But why do you go?" Mia had asked. "Why don't you tell them what you feel?"

"I don't know . . . it's stupid . . . not to say cowardly. But I don't want to hurt them."

Mia had told him about Gran and the old people's home and all the old ladies in flowered prints sitting together busying themselves with Christmas presents for their grandchildren. And what Gran had said about the most important thing being the feeling that you had someone who cared that you were alive.

"And she's got four children," said Mia. "Think of the ones with no children." As the words came out of her mouth, there was a twinge in that chrysalis down there, but at that moment a log fell off the fire and suddenly they had something else to do.

It wasn't until they were just about to leave that Mia once again stepped outside her role.

"Jan," she said, as she stood in the hall buttoning up her coat. "I've been thinking. Even if it's not certain after all, I'd still like to know more . . . about this. I mean . . . about abortion and everything. What it's all about and what different people think and so on. I think I could find out all about it at the library—we've done that kind of thing in group work at school, you know. There's lots of stuff in magazines and reference books—couldn't you come with me? We could go to the city library in Stockholm and read together, couldn't we . . . wouldn't that be a good thing?"

"Well . . . yes, of course it'd be good . . . but . . ."

"Are you busy?" she asked quickly.

"Well, you wouldn't know, but our club's playing in Västerås both tomorrow and on Sunday. I didn't know this . . . I mean, I arranged ages ago that Leif and I would go, and we'd stay with Leif's sister, who's married and lives there. Don't think I'm being awkward, but . . ."

"Oh," said Mia, laughing, feeling far too calm and happy to be disappointed just then. "Of course you must go. I'll tell you about it later."

"Great," said Jan, brightening, his gratitude so extensive and palpable that Mia's cap fell off and a button got torn off her coat.

Mia smiled to herself as she thought about it.

"I love him," she said to herself. "Terribly."

And the elevator flew like a rosy cloud up toward the seventh floor.

Has everyone gone to bed already? she thought as she stepped into the hall. It's not even eleven yet.

The door to the bedroom was closed and there was no light on in the kitchen. Strange . . . She stood listening intently and heard a slight rustle of paper from the living room.

She pushed open the door and stood in the doorway.

"Hello, Mia," her father said, getting up out of the armchair and letting the newspaper fall to the floor. "Did you have a good time?"

"Yes, lovely," Mia said mechanically. Her eyes flew from her father's face to the bedclothes lying thrown on the sofa. "Are . . . are you sleeping out here, Dad?"

"Yes, your mother's . . . she's got a cold and is tired, so she thought it'd be best," he said, beginning to fumble about with the blankets without looking at her.

"I'll help you make the bed up," said Mia, hearing how thin and trembly her own voice sounded. "Are you so childish that you think I'll believe that?" she wanted to say. "I know perfectly well Mother hasn't got a cold." Suddenly all her suppressed anxiety rushed up inside her again. She felt like throwing her handbag down on to the floor and shouting: *"I can't stand your troubles too!"* But she neither threw down her bag nor shouted. Instead she said in a calm voice: "You hold the sheet there and then we can tuck it in here and put two chairs in front—like that—and now the blankets."

"Thanks, Mia poppet, that's good of you," said Dad, his voice heartrendingly cheerful. "That'll be fine. Thanks. Off you go to bed now, darling. You've had a long day."

His kiss brushed against her cheek, but he was looking beyond her.

"Night, Dad, and sleep well," said Mia, picking up her bag and rushing for the door so that her father wouldn't hear how the tears were welling up and thickening her voice.

"Sleep well, poppet."

Sleep well. Oh, God.

The Advent candlestick, with its polished brass and four unlit white candles, was standing in the middle of the table when Mia staggered out into the kitchen at about half past ten on Saturday morning.

Mia stared at it with distaste.

If only it weren't Christmas.

It was more than she could bear that it was *Christmas* in the middle of all this awful mess, when everything should be fun and busy and secretive.

The smell of gingerbread, cutting out shiny new paper hearts, the big straw goat, hyacinths on the low table, decorating the ham with sugar mixture through a cone, all the presents in the basket . . . "Silent Night" and "Hark! the Herald Angels . . ."

She sank down at the table and leaned her head against

the cool oilcloth; all those things that had been exciting and fun only last year.

Suddenly as she sat there, she realized how completely silent it was in the apartment. Everyone had already gone out. At the same instant she noticed a pad lying by the bread bin with something written on it in her mother's handwriting. Lillan and she had been invited to Aunt Vera's for Pelle's birthday party. He was nine. Perhaps they'd stay the night, she had written. Dad had gone to see Gran but would be home in the afternoon. There was food in the refrigerator. Love and kisses.

Mia felt almost shamefully relieved that Mother and Lillan were to be away for the weekend. Now she wouldn't have to act and be happy for Advent for Lillan's sake; wouldn't have to see Mother's eyes when she looked at Dad, or avoided looking at him, or hear their tone of voice.

Then she could go into Stockholm to the city library and read all day if she wanted to.

It was good that Jan was away too, really. They couldn't have gone on pretending, as they had last night, for two whole days. In the long run, they would finally have had an argument.

Instead she could now come back for dinner and pretend a little with poor Dad, eat the grilling chicken that was in the refrigerator, watch TV, chat, and not think. And then take two aspirins and hope for a better night than last night. It had been awful.

She'd lain awake, twisting and turning in the sheets right up until about five o'clock. Now and again she'd fallen into a horrible state of semiconsciousness full of strange dreams which were even worse than consciousness; horrible dreams about horses and embryos and chemical formulas and Mother throwing bricks at Dad.

Heavens, she'd almost forgotten that she had to take a sample to the drugstore today—strange that she should nearly forget that. As long as she could find another little bottle—and what had she done with that paper she'd had from the druggist the day before yesterday?

Mia ran back into her bedroom and began rummaging in her handbag. A green paper? Yes, there it was. What did it say now? *Information on Pregnancy Tests.*

The urine sample should be taken in the morning of the day it is handed in. The sample should be in a glass vessel which has been thoroughly cleaned or the test may be faulty. Oh, yes, *after cleaning, the vessel should be well rinsed out with water, as even small quantities of detergents or disinfectants can affect the result.* That's what she'd done wrong, of course. *Your identity number should be written on the label on the bottle. No test method is a hundred per cent reliable. To arrive at the best possible results, however, it is important that samples be given according to the above instructions.* Yes, she'd wash and rinse it all right this time. If only she could find a little bottle now . . . she could hardly take a liter bottle.

An operation for abortion differs from other surgical treatment in that it gives rise to various moral and ethical judgments. Conclusions come to when such judg-

ments are made as a basis for one's own decision are arbitrary.

Mia frowned and read that sentence again.

The risk of sub . . . subjectivity in the individual hospital doctor's decision is in other words so much greater in the case of abortion than in the case of other operations. Society should therefore not allow the question of operation to be a matter solely between the woman and the responsible doctor, but should give directions for abortions . . .

And again: *The risk of subjectivity . . .*

Mia sat curled up at a table at the far end of the reading room, reading several books at once.

At first she'd felt terribly confused, not knowing where to go or whom to ask. She'd never been to the city library before and when she'd climbed up the great steps and gone into the huge, circular book-lined room, where a number of librarians were working behind a desk in the middle, at first she'd been so shocked that she'd almost forgotten what she had come for.

It was so unlike the library at home in the shopping center, which was new and light and polished and cream-colored, with enormous windows, while this was dark and sheltered, imposing in some way . . . like some kind of temple for books or a fort or something . . . as if you were in a huge drum clad in red spines of books . . . some kind of sacred room where people wandered around, silent and tranquil, worshiping the printed word. You felt awe just from the smell.

At first she'd just walked around the circular room enjoying the atmosphere. It had felt like a refuge . . . as if Life, which was such a trouble, was a long way away.

Then a kindly librarian had come and asked if she could be of any help, and now Mia was sitting there, her table cluttered with books and newspaper clippings, chewing alternately on a banana and a bar of chocolate as she leafed through the books and read and read and leafed through more books. Her hair kept falling over her face and she kept frowning heavily. Why do people write things in such a complicated way?

In an old notebook she'd brought from home she wrote down extracts from what she thought was more important. For and against, for and against . . .

The Commission dissociates itself from the statement that treatment of this kind of a woman should be legalized as a new method of birth control—i.e., as a new contraceptive. With consideration of the risks to health and the strain of an operation, men and women should not rely on abortion except in an emergency. . . .

The abortion question is a matter of conscience. It is neither natural nor defensible—as happens in thoughts on abortion—to ignore the admittedly traditional but also natural and necessary principle that sexual intercourse involves responsibility. . . .

All that about responsibility must be right, whether you're a Christian or not. When someone is pregnant, there's always a lot of responsibility involved sooner or later. Either you accept it or you don't. You didn't have to be a bishop to understand that. It's just that you discover it too late!

If women are to be granted the right to abortion, then they should also be granted the right to give birth, wrote Doctor Elisabeth Sjövall. *They should be offered such social and financial benefits that they have a free choice in the matter. It has earlier been said that legal abortion preserves social ills. That is no less true today.*

But schoolgirls then—are they also women who have a free choice through social and financial benefits?

. . . the fewer sustained motives women have had for abortion, the greater the risk of regrets later on. Negative reactions after an abortion are more common in women who have been exposed to influences from husbands or others surrounding them, women who themselves would have preferred to have given birth to the child.

But the man then? Like Jan—if he's forced to—doesn't anyone bother about that? *It is also worth noting that the Commission has completely ignored the biological father's legal position.*

But he has to pay.

A woman cannot be more alone with her conscience than with abortion on demand. The moment a woman is declared "the chooser," then the man is relieved of all responsibility— In practice the woman's will is already the decisive factor. Refusals nearly always occur only when the woman is hesitant or when she really only wants a refusal to show her relations. Such liberal practice implies in reality that women are exposed to undue influences from their relations.

Undue influences . . . Mia read the piece again.

But when was influence undue? Who should decide

that? If parents influence a fifteen-year-old girl—who'd become pregnant by an unknown boy—to have an abortion, can that be called undue influence?

Then it must be just as undue influence if a strange doctor, who happens to be religious, decides that a woman must keep the child.

It was difficult. Mia sat staring straight ahead of her, chewing absentmindedly on a piece of chocolate. There was so much complicated reasoning that she could hardly understand. For instance, what that archbishop had said: *According to Christian-inspired thinking, one sees man's authority as a means—without damaging one's own life—of depriving the merciless struggle for existence of some of its dominion and allowing one ethical principle embraced by mankind to regulate life on earth.* What did that mean then?

Anyway, it didn't make any difference. She could grasp that if you're a Christian then you think in a different way from those who aren't, and you didn't have to be a Christian to think that naturally it's better if you never get into a situation involving considering abortion. But that was simple!

And clearly it was not something you did just for fun. Anyhow, late abortions seemed horrible. *Women should choose abortion rather than contraceptives, they say,* wrote an angry young woman journalist in one clipping. *If anyone believes that, it proves that they know nothing. Abortion is no fun.*

Mia shivered. It was strange sitting here reading about these vital and burning questions in this huge silent room, with its smell of old paper, its neat little labels for different subjects, its quiet visitors. . . . By the dark window opposite the entrance was a dusty climbing plant, and the hands of the great clock in the corner moved silently around its mustard-yellow face.

It was already past four— Dad would be home long ago and perhaps wondering where she was. No, he'd think she was going to be with Jan all day. Suppose she called him and said she'd be home for dinner? She didn't have to tell him she'd been sitting in the city library reading about abortions.

Dad sounded so pleased when Mia said she'd be back for dinner that she felt a lump come into her throat and was forced to cough.

"Then I'll go down to the bakery and get a small princess gateau, so we can have a treat with our coffee," he said.

"Only a *very* small one, then," laughed Mia.

Princess gateau was the best treat she knew: the real thing with layers of vanilla cream in between and a thick layer of whipped cream under the marzipan.

She went through the books and papers one last time. Should she borrow any of them to take home?

No, she wouldn't. She wasn't much the wiser from all this anyway. She'd really known all the time—though only just rather dimly inside her—how fearfully complicated it was and at the same time how self-evident . . . a necessary development.

She glanced in Hertha for the last time. *In contrast to many other matters of principle which the Frederika*

Bremer Society works for, complete unity has not been reached on this question. A clear majority both in groups and among individual members who have expressed opinions has, however, voted for abortion on demand after obligatory advice. A considerable increase in social benefit resources is also generally demanded.

That sounded sensible.

And yet she would most of all have liked to talk to a human being. Some wise, experienced adult person.

Mia had a headache and her eyes were smarting with fatigue when she left the library, her notebook full of notes and her crumpled paper bag full of banana peel and chocolate wrappings.

Her brain was whirling with complicated words and arguments—ethical analysis—liberal practice—the sanctity of life—standpoints of principle—humanitarian abortion indication . . .

She decided to walk to the bus stop instead of going by subway. Dad wasn't expecting her home for a while. She drew in a deep breath before running down the broad steps.

It was lovely weather, cold and fresh, but not bitter, small dry snowflakes swirling around in the air and falling on her hair and fur collar. The street glittered with Christmas lights and all the stores had already arranged their Christmas presents between cotton and Christmas elves and red rosettes.

It was the first Sunday in Advent tomorrow.

As Mia pushed her way through the stream of people walking by, she felt for the first time that year a trace of happy expectation at the thought of Christmas.

All those robes and hockey sticks and toy trains and fur gloves and ovenware and silver shoes floated before her eyes behind the bright windows. In broken Swedish, a frozen street seller tried to persuade her to buy some of the fragile silver-like jewelry he had spread out on the sidewalk. Someone was laboriously picking out "A White Christmas" on a guitar. In the fruit store on the corner, fat marzipan pigs were wedged between heaps of walnuts and boxes of dates. The movie on the other side of the street was showing Donald Duck's latest Christmas adventure. The travel bureau was offering the Canary Islands in the Christmas sunshine beneath a garland of pine sprays.

It was only just over three weeks to Christmas. Everything was as usual.

Suddenly Mia was the little girl she'd been so recently. She allowed herself to be gripped by the wonderful old childhood enchantment of Christmas, when you counted the days and wrote present lists on old paper bags and dreamed of long white skates and a new Barbie doll and the latest Beatle record and half worried yourself to death over how twenty-three kronor fifty would stretch around presents for seven people.

Dad had set the table, candles and all, when Mia got back, and the chicken lay beautifully divided on a dish. There was a delicious smell of frying potatoes, and he had even got out a bottle of red wine.

Mia wasn't all that fond of red wine, but she appreciated the gesture, which meant that now she was almost a grown young woman, dining with her father on chicken and red wine.

"How beautifully you've done it all," she said, kissing him on the ear.

"The gateau's still in the refrigerator."

"What a time we're going to have. It all looks wonderful and you've got some of that jelly, too. Where did you find that?"

"Right at the back of the pantry. Well, now, we're all ready to go, I think," said Dad, undoing the apron. "Please be seated, young lady." He pulled out a chair for Mia and pushed it in again for her.

So they played the pretending game.

It was as if the world didn't exist outside this cozy spot, smelling of rosemary, melted butter, and candles, the red wine in the best glasses glimmering in a friendly way in the candlelight, helping them with their game.

They chatted and laughed and enjoyed being fond of each other and having the same nose and the same chin and the same color of hair; and yet they both knew it was a game, though Mia knew more about it than her father.

The pleasant atmosphere lasted right through coffee and gateau, which they had in the living room, Dad in his armchair and Mia lolling on the sofa, groaning with repletion.

Afterward, she couldn't really say when the game suddenly came to an end. Perhaps it began with the news on the radio dampening their cheerfulness. Perhaps it was when Mia happened to look up and see her father's face, naked, when he didn't know she was looking. She at once saw how tired and unhappy he looked as he sat there, his thin hair brushed carefully across his bald head, the stalwart black sideburns simply making his pale thin cheeks look even more middle-aged.

They both sat in silence, for suddenly there was nothing to talk about. Mia felt a little sick and a headache began to creep up on her. Dad lit a cigarette but put it out almost at once. Suddenly he got up and went across to the window. The sky was clear and dark blue, thousands of stars competing with Lillan's handsome Datema.

Perhaps that was what brought reality back.

"Mia," he said roughly, turning around to face her. "I've got to talk to you about something . . . I didn't mean to do it now, but . . ."

"I know, Dad."

"You know? Has Mother . . .?"

"No, she hasn't said anything. But I . . . I've . . . I've known all the same. Are you getting a divorce?" As she asked the question, she realized coldly and clearly what the words meant, what the reality behind the words involved, and she could feel the tears coming.

"No . . . not divorce . . . Mia . . . not yet, anyway. But

we're going to try living apart for a while . . . to see if . . . if that helps. We can't go on like this." He went back to the armchair and sank down into it, his head in his hands. "Things have gone wrong in some way. We just misunderstand each other and hurt each other."

"How are you going to arrange it, then?" Mia asked, trying to sound calm and matter-of-fact.

"Well, you see . . . we'd thought . . . we've talked a lot about it. And I must tell you it's not the first time we've agreed to live apart for a while. We did the same once many years ago, but nothing came of it. It turned out that Mother was expecting Lillan.

"Well," he went on, "we thought we'd do this . . . Mother'll take Lillan and go home to Halland for a while. Not now, of course, but after Christmas."

"To Halland? But . . . her job . . . and her studies—what about them?"

"Well, you see, the job'll come to an end anyway. You probably haven't heard yet, but the store's closing and the staff is being given notice on January first."

"What nerve . . . suddenly, just like that!"

"It's not quite so sudden as it seems. It's difficult to keep that kind of small handicrafts shop going nowadays."

"But Lillan's school. And the riding school?"

"Well, there's a school down there near Grandpa's place and she'll have horses on the farm, so she'll be delighted.

"And you and I . . . Mia," Dad said, raising his head and smiling a little crookedly. "You and I will have to try to console each other for a while. Do you think . . . do you think we can manage?"

Mia didn't reply. She was sitting up dead straight on the sofa, staring out the window, feeling as if someone had hit her very hard on the head, as if the ceiling had fallen down. Of course she'd known that things weren't right between her mother and father. Of course the thought that they might separate had flown through her, especially lately.

But she'd never let that thought sink in.

It had never been a reality.

It was just like death—it couldn't happen in our family. Or like becoming pregnant against your will—it couldn't happen to me. And yet it had happened. It had happened to Mother and Dad. It had perhaps happened to her.

Mia turned to look at her father without really seeing him. She couldn't get a word out. Everything whirled around, in her head, in her heart. She suddenly felt how, deep down inside her, rage was beginning to grow. A strange fury. Mostly about Mother . . . Mother who'd betrayed her, who'd just gone off with Lillan. They could at least have asked her before deciding anything. What a way to behave, just deciding things over your head!

"Mia . . ." She saw her father's pleading expression in the reddish lamplight. "Don't you think it'd work? It's just a tryout—for a term at the most. And I promise you it won't be a burden to you. . . . I'll be . . . domestic." He laughed uncertainly.

"Perhaps if you'd tried to help *Mother* a bit more before, then this needn't have happened," said Mia, rather sharply.

"Mia, dear . . . it's much more complicated than that.

What was cause and what effect we don't even know ourselves."

But Mia wasn't listening to his answer. She was just sitting there, making a huge effort to grasp all the confusing and violent and desperate feelings that were welling up inside her.

This wasn't like being scared and desperate because perhaps you were pregnant.

This was worse. As if someone had cut away the foundations of her own actual security in life.

But it was no surprise. She had thought about it before. Gran had hinted things to her.

But that didn't help. Now it had been said. Now it was irretrievable. Not only that Mother and Dad weren't fond of each other and wanted to live apart . . . but they'd behaved and thought like this for ages, almost all of Mia's childhood, all the years she'd lived with them and laughed and talked and eaten and done her homework and celebrated Christmas and birthdays and gone on outings and kissed and hugged. All that time was like one great betrayal; a pretending game that she'd never seen through, a security which was totally hollow.

"Then why didn't you get divorced *before,*" she cried suddenly, her anger threatening to blow her into small pieces. "Why have you gone on cheating all the time, pretending and pretending?"

"But, Mia, dear . . ." Dad looked anxiously at her. "We thought that . . . that it was for your sake."

"For our sake . . . we've never asked for any false pretense of happiness."

"But, Mia . . ." Dad made a helpless gesture. "We've

always tried to do what we thought best. What else could we have done? One does what one can. . . ."

"You should never have gotten married, Gran said."

"Oh, is that what she says? Well, it's easy to be wise after the event."

He drew the back of his hand across his eyes and suddenly Mia could see again and saw that her father was weeping. The fury within her subsided like a wave. What had she done?

"Oh, Dad, I'm sorry. I'm so mixed up I don't know what I'm saying . . . I'm *sorry*." She rushed up off the sofa and knelt down beside him. "Dad, don't cry . . . it'll be all right, you'll see . . . you and me . . ."

Dad blew his nose and patted her shoulder. "It's you who should be forgiving me," he mumbled.

"What do you mean, Dad?" Mia stayed on the floor, holding her father's hand against her cheek, which was also wet with tears. "Am I supposed to forgive you because you're not happy, or what?"

He smiled slightly and stroked her cheek.

"You haven't been all that happy yourself lately, have you, Mia darling?" he said finally. "I think I've known that all along."

"I thought you and Mother had enough on your plate," she mumbled, different longings struggling within her.

Of course she couldn't say anything *now* . . . before it was definite. That'd be crazy. And yet at the same time great. To be able to talk to someone grown up. And also—if she were pregnant, what about Mother and Dad's plans for the spring?

Before she could get around to deciding which she

should do, she heard her father's voice, saying a little cautiously:

"Is it . . . I know it's nothing to do with me . . . but are you having trouble with Jan?"

"It depends on what you mean by trouble, Dad," she heard herself say. "You see . . . you see . . . perhaps . . . I may be pregnant." The tears came welling up. "But . . . but . . ." she hiccuped, "it's n-not abs-s-solutely c-c-certain."

At first her father said nothing, just letting her cry, stroking her head gently.

"You poor old thing, you," he said in the end. "And then we go and pour all our own troubles on top of you as well."

"I'll know on Monday," Mia said, wiping her face on her father's trouser leg.

"And . . . what does Jan say?"

"He wants to get married right away."

"And what do you want?"

"I don't want to . . . to get married now. What do you think? The worst thing is . . . he can't . . . you know his father's a minister, and now he says . . . he says he can't even consider my having it taken away."

"And what about you?" Dad's voice sounded terribly serious and Mia swallowed repeatedly before she spoke.

"Well, I think I want to, Dad. But we must talk about it properly first."

"Of course we'll talk about it, Mia darling, and you mustn't worry more than necessary, promise me that. Of course your mother and I'll help you in every way."

"In what way?"

"In whatever way you want yourself, darling."

Mia pulled a cushion off the sofa and lay down on the rug at her father's feet. She suddenly felt dead tired, as if someone had turned her inside out and just left the peel behind.

The room lay in the half-light. Dad had lit a cigarette and was slowly blowing large smoke rings, which gradually floated up to the ceiling. It was restful.

"Are you tired?"

"Yes, dead tired." She pushed the cushion further up under her head.

The next minute she was asleep.

Her father was the only one to hear the consoling sound of the ten thin strokes from the concrete church.

Hark! the Herald Angels sing
Glory to the newborn king;
Peace on earth and mercy mild,
God and sinners reconciled. . . .

Mia slowly came to life.

The neighbor's radio was booming through her wall.

She didn't move; just lay there with her eyes closed, taking in the familiar tune, allowing herself to be gripped by all the jubilation and memories and expectations it implied. At that moment nothing else existed except the powerful, beautiful music ringing with joy. As long as it continued there was no yesterday, no tomorrow, no problems. No reality, no pretense, only a soft warm nest of memories.

For a long while after the carol was over, Mia lay still. She'd slept for so long and so deeply and dreamlessly that she needed time to climb out of the well. Reality, standing at the side of her bed, waiting for her to wake up and face it, was so complex that she didn't know which anxiety she should allow in first. She didn't even bother to check as usual whether anything had happened in the night. She just lay flat on her back and let herself rise slowly to the surface.

Suddenly she noticed that her nightgown was on back to front and she wondered how she'd got to bed. She realized, too, that there was a reddish glow penetrating her eyelids and she wondered what time it was. When she carefully opened her eyes, she saw that the blind had not been drawn down and the slanting winter sunlight was making a sunny patch on the ceiling. And all the sounds from outside had that clear light tone that they have in the winter when the weather is fine.

It should have been a hateful day to wake up to.

A day when she knew Mother and Dad were to separate, another day when she *didn't* know whether she was pregnant, a day when Jan was far away, yelling at a lot of foolish handball players, and Mother was probably sitting on Aunt Vera's sofa, crying and telling her about the separation; a day when you didn't know what expression would be in Dad's eyes and what you should talk about at breakfast.

A rotten day when the weather should be foul so that you could hide yourself indoors and read magazines and eat princess gateau and try not to think.

And then the sun shone and things hummed with joy, hope, and expectation.

There was a knock on the door.

"Come in."

It was Dad standing there with a tray and coffee and candles.

"Oh, Dad, how wonderful."

"Well, you see, I thought we could have it in here and then we could take the car and go out for a drive. It's such fantastic weather out . . . two degrees of frost and brilliant sun. And I think we both need a bit of air. Perhaps we could go to some place for lunch . . . then we can make the most of the time . . . what do you think? If you'd like to, of course. But you said yesterday that Jan wouldn't be home until this evening."

"Oh, Dad . . . that'd be terrific."

They didn't say much to each other on the trip through their suburb. There were a lot of people out and around in the fine weather and heavy traffic heading toward Stockholm. Not until they'd passed the huge new high-rise area on the other side of the railroad did Mia's father break the silence.

"You know, this is where we had our allotment when I was small."

"Here?"

"Yes, there was a large area of allotments here with lots

of tiny cottages. It was the only summer vacation hundreds of people had in those days."

"Summer vacation here . . . right by the railroad."

"You have to remember that most workers had no vacation when I was a child. In 1931, when I was seven, the first laws were passed giving four days' vacation to a worker who'd been a long time with the same employer . . . and the law giving two weeks' vacation didn't come in until 1938, I think."

"Gosh," mumbled Mia, thinking about all her vacations with Granny and Grandpa in Halland.

"So it was great then to have an allotment cottage. Mom and Dad used to bike out there nearly every evening in the summer, and for long spells when it was fine weather, Mom used to stay there with us kids. They worked like slaves on the allotment and dug and planted and ridged potatoes and harvested the apples. I can still smell the autumn smell of apples all over the cottage—apples and kerosene. Mom sold flowers to passers-by—asters and goldenrod and rudbeckias and tall . . . what are they called—gladiolas."

"It sounds nice. Like living in a play house."

"That's just about what it looked like, too—red with white shutters and a tiny veranda, where you sat and drank coffee when the sun was out. And Mom wove special small rag rugs which would fit the room. In August we had a crayfish party and colored lanterns."

"Crayfish? That are so expensive?"

"Not then—those were different days. You bought them off some friends who'd been out poaching somewhere in the country."

Mia sat silent for a moment.

"It's funny," she said finally. "Everything seems so different as soon as it belongs to the past. I mean—either great fun and idyllic or else just awful."

"Yes," her father said slowly, braking to turn off on to a forest road. "Yes, that's it—the truth's as slippery as an eel. Mostly one needs to gild the past a little, console oneself, boast a little, perhaps. Though sometimes it's the other way around. One needs to blacken it, make people and circumstances appear worse than they were, as if to defend oneself."

He sat silent again. "That business of seeing through one's own motives I think is one of the most difficult things to do," he said in the end.

"I'd . . . I'd awfully like to know," said Mia, "what you and Mother were like when you were children and young. I mean what you thought and liked and were afraid of and believed and all that . . . what you thought was fun and so on. But even if you tell me, it's sort of . . . sort of only a little bit of the truth, isn't it?"

"Yes, indeed, that's true. And the worst thing is that one doesn't know much about oneself either, who one was, how one became what one is . . . and why. Was it something within oneself—inborn—or was it circumstances?"

Mia didn't know what to say and realized that he was thinking about himself and her mother. Perhaps about his work too. Perhaps Gran had been right.

The road became narrower and full of potholes and the countryside grew more and more beautiful, so much so that it hurt.

It had been such a long time since Mia had bothered with outdoor things, she'd almost forgotten that the sun almost forces you to be a little happy. Though that wasn't quite true, of course, because only the other day it'd been fine weather and then she'd hated the sun and the rime frost and everything.

But at the moment her own worries were sufficiently suppressed and becalmed that she was able to find time for the beauty around her.

It was strange that everything got more beautiful when the sun was low, when the rays fell slantingly from below and conjured up colors and fine warm shadows. It was also strange that it was almost more beautiful when the leaves had fallen and the trees were left standing naked against the sky, although the minute before you'd thought that the red and gold of autumn was best of all, even better than the summer and spring.

Suddenly all this black and white was stunningly beautiful, small clumps of birches like pen-and-ink drawings on the edge of a patchy field, where the snow lay like icing sugar on chocolate-brown clods of earth, a crowd of black jackdaws against a cold pale-blue background.

"Do you want to leave the car here and walk now?" her father said, drawing up to the side of the road.

They turned off along a path into a small area of mixed woodland, the ground slippery with pine needles and roots, the leaves crackling in the frost.

"How fantastically beautiful it is here," said Mia. The air was full of the smell of damp and pine trees. "What heavenly colors . . . just when you think there are no colors at this time of year. Amazing how subtle it all is."

And then suddenly among the browns and grays they could see an emerald-green cushion of moss on a stone, a few red hips-and-haws on a thorny rosebush, a lot of tangled yellow horsetail among the lingonberry plants.

A patch of water winked between the trees.

They walked slowly in that direction, Dad breaking off a long smooth aspen switch, Mia picking some long-dead goldenrod. They walked and then sat down on an abandoned bathing jetty. A thin membrane of ice covered the lake, making it look like a great stainless steel mirror. Mia longed to go down to the edge and feel the crunch of it under the sole of her boots.

But she didn't move.

The sun warmed their faces, making Dad's pale face look ruddy and healthy. He looked so young in his Russian fur cap, when you didn't notice the sparse graying hair and the lines on his forehead.

They sat silently and let the sun do its conjuring tricks, letting themselves be consoled and warmed. Mia's eyes flitted around and took in the beauty of the countryside, pretending that she was writing an essay in her head—"One Day in Winter."

A late larch tree, which has not yet lost its needles, sticks its mustard-yellow bottle brushes up through the dark confusion of the undergrowth of alder. Snowberry bushes, a flying wild duck in spool-shaped silhouette against . . . against . . . No, what rubbish.

She laughed and looked up at her father, who had just got up.

"Well, I think we'd better not sit here any longer and get chilled—that's enough nature worship for one day."

"Funny, isn't it," mumbled Mia. "This place just lies here and does nothing but be beautiful day after day, though we don't see it."

They turned their backs on the lake and began to walk briskly up toward the road. The sun had already begun to sink down toward the pine tree skyline in the southwest and the warmth in the air quickly receded. The colors of the forest had already been extinguished by the time they had reached the car.

How quickly it went, thought Mia in astonishment, and she shivered.

Suddenly it was as if all her anxiety had also come to life again and begun to stir, just as last night when the good atmosphere at dinner had suddenly gone.

Walking here, boggling at the sun and the snowberries, when there are so many more important things to talk about.

But it wasn't until they'd eaten their pork and applesauce and Brussels sprouts and vanilla ice cream with peaches at Sätra Guest House that Mia plucked up her courage. There weren't many guests and the motherly waitress had left them in peace with their coffee. Outside the multipaned old windows the darkness had begun to fall. A large red Advent star swung slowly like a deformed starfish in the heat from the Advent candles. There were some sweet-smelling pine branches in a brass tub in the open fireplace.

It was all so desperately cozy.

"Dad . . ."

"Yes?"

"Dad . . . I'd . . . I'd like to know what you . . . what your attitude is about . . . about abortion." Against her will she'd lowered her voice on the last word.

Her father sat silently for a moment, drawing on his cigarette.

"Well, you know," he said, looking seriously straight at her, "I don't think I can give you one answer to that question."

"But you aren't against abortion on demand, are you?" said Mia, leaning forward. "I thought once . . . once last year, when you and Mother were talking about the new laws, you sounded . . . I thought you sounded as if you didn't agree when she said it was obvious that a woman should be allowed to decide when and if she wanted children."

"If I remember rightly—and I remember that occasion quite well for other reasons—all I said then was that it wasn't that simple."

"What do you mean?"

"Well, I mean that I think too that in principle it's right that a woman shouldn't have to give birth to children except when she herself wants to. And . . . at the same time it's . . . it's a damned complicated business. I think the number of abortions last year was pretty frightening—even if they haven't increased lately so much as they'd expected."

"But that's because so many people were frightened of the pill, isn't it?"

"Exactly—that's what's wrong—they haven't done the

preliminaries very successfully, for abortion on demand wasn't meant to be used as a new kind of contraceptive. The Abortion Commission emphasized that too."

"Yes, I know. No, thank you, no more coffee."

The motherly waitress had come back with more coffee. She was hovering around the table as long as she could, snuffing out a candle that was smoking, sweeping away some invisible crumbs. Mia could see the curiosity shining in her eyes—what exactly was going on between this ill-matched pair?

Mia was certain that she'd gone out to the kitchen to the cook and huffed and puffed about middle-aged men enticing out young girls who were hardly of age. Mia sighed impatiently. Now she'd forgotten what she was going to say. The old grandfather clock in the corner struck four—soon they'd have to go home.

"But, Dad, you said before that in principle it's right to have abortions on demand, and then you say at the same time that you can't give one answer to that question."

Again her father thought for a while before answering.

"Well, one answer is perhaps the wrong way of putting it. But I find it difficult to express what I feel. And neither have I had any reason to look into the question properly, even if I have talked to quite a number of people in the party about it—a social worker, among others. I suppose I reacted against those who wanted to simplify the problem too much. After all, it's not just like going to have a tooth out, is it? I mean . . ."

He stopped, searching for the right words.

He's afraid of scaring me, thought Mia.

". . . there's still so much emotionalism tied up with abortion. Conscience and guilt and things like that. And apart from the purely religious aspects . . . all that diffuse talk about the right to life and obey God before people or sentimental harangues about 'politics that are hostile to life, which sacrifice the smallest ones, those not yet visible to our eyes,' as I read the other day."

"That's what Jan's parents think," interrupted Mia.

"Well, one has to respect the fact that there are people who feel and think like that. But that doesn't mean that their values should be imposed on others. But apart from all that . . ."

"Yes?"

". . . you really can't get away from the fact that it's one of the most important matters to humankind—this business of children or no children. It's relevant to the actual principle of life—the whole reproduction instinct—all our concepts of what we call . . . happiness. It's not so peculiar that there's been such a lot of discussion on the question of abortion, and also, naturally, it's very important it doesn't become unnecessarily complicated—that you try to look at it soberly and factually from case to case."

"And then," said Mia, "you open a magazine and read about a girl who's thrilled to pieces she didn't obey her fiancé and have an abortion and who's now alone at home with her sweet little baby and is the happiest creature on earth."

Dad smiled wryly. "Exactly—that's what I mean. You can never get away from all these triumphant testimonials —because when a child is born, then it is often loved against all odds. But whether it then gets a secure childhood and a reasonable chance in life—that's quite another matter."

"Yes," said Mia hesitantly. "Maybe the most important thing is that you try to see that a child has what it needs from the beginning, not that it must be born at any price? Though it's difficult to know what's right for it. That can change, can't it?"

"Speculating on whether it would've been better if a person had been born or not is pretty pointless," said her father. "There are always contradictory cases, thank heavens—the poor invalid who becomes a wealthy and happy explorer or the spoiled rich man's son who commits suicide in wretchedness, et cetera. That's why I think the Christian's talk about the right to live for every embryo also seems so meaningless—you might just as well care about every ovum that goes to waste."

"You mean you should be concerned with the gir . . . the woman?"

"It must be the living person who comes first and what she wants to do with her life."

"But if . . . she does the wrong things?"

"Oh, Mia, everyone's always taking the risk of doing the wrong thing. You can only do what you think is right and true *at that moment,* don't you think?"

Dad lit another cigarette, his hand trembling slightly.

"Unfortunately life's full of things that go wrong."

"You mean—with you and Mother?"

"Yes. We thought we were doing the only right thing when we got married, when you were on the way. For me it was quite obvious, because I loved Marianne and very much wanted to get married. I had a good job and was nearly thirty."

"And Mother?"

"Well, she was so young—but I think she was in love with me then. Anyway, there was no alternative. Abortion was out of the question and your grandmother was very eager for us to get married. Unwed mothers were certainly not the fashion in those days," he said, smiling a little.

"And when I think about you children—then it can't be anything else but right, you must see that. What would my life be without you and Lillan? And of course your mother feels that way about you too. And yet . . ." He stopped and looked past Mia at the wall behind her. "It went wrong. Mother was too young."

"But, Dad, maybe you'd have gotten married even if you hadn't been expecting me. Perhaps it would've gone wrong anyway."

"Maybe. Maybe it should never have been us two but I think the chances of it's going well would have been far greater if your mother had finished her education and had had time to start a job. Mother just isn't the kind who is suited to being just a housewife, but I didn't realize that until it was too late."

"Do you think any girls are suited to being just housewives?"

"I wouldn't like to express an opinion on that, Mia. I've probably been too old-fashioned. But every generation has its starting points. I was proud of the fact that I had such a good job that my wife didn't have to work herself to the bone, as my mother had had to. Right or wrong—who decides that and when? Today—yesterday—in a hundred years' time—or . . ."

"You really can't argue like that, Dad," interrupted Mia.

Her father made no reply. He sat twisting his wedding ring around and around and suddenly seemed to have forgotten Mia's presence. She didn't bother to pick up the thread. The silence grew heavy this time and Mia realized her father's thoughts were far away. She felt slightly forsaken. How would she be able to say what she wanted to say? The dining room was quite empty now, only a gray tabby cat sneaking around the tables looking for something to eat. Mia's eyes strayed around the room. On the wall above her father's seat was an embroidered sampler.

When I was fifteen
the cottage grew small
where I lived
with my mother

It was embroidered in red stem stitch, surrounded by an elaborate wreath of roses.

Mia recognized the sampler—Granny had one just like it in her spare room; a silly thing to have on the wall.

Between the windows were two colored portraits of a fat old king covered with orders and a fat queen in light blue puffed sleeves.

There was a smell of frying onions from the kitchen. Someone laughed shrilly and long.

Mia shivered, suddenly longing desperately for Jan.

"But Mia, dear," she heard her father saying, "we've never gotten around to your views on abortion. The most important thing is what you think yourself."

"We—ell," said Mia, twisting her table napkin. "I think that one should decide oneself, too, if one can . . ."

Mia watched the gray cat, as she struggled to find the right words.

". . . I read in the paper about a woman journalist who got really angry about postponing the laws—she seemed to think it was a kind of vote of no confidence in women —that they weren't mature enough to take responsibility for what they did. And she's right in a way, but . . ."

"Yes?"

"Not all women are mature and wise and sensible and know exactly what they're doing. And even if they're adult and married and everything, they're obviously often forced into abortion by their husbands, even when they don't want it. So what about girls of my age and younger—who should decide for them? How can they really know what they want, Dad? And if they want something definite, then maybe it's wrong. I read that it's nearly always the youngest and most immature who want to keep their children—a doll to play with—something which is all their very own."

Mia gulped down some coffee, which tasted foul.

"And Barbro told me about a girl she knew, a young girl of fifteen, whose parents persuaded her to have an abortion, although she herself said she didn't want one. And afterward she started taking drugs and running around at night and now she blames her parents—says it's because she wasn't allowed to keep her child. I suppose she could've just made all that up, but if she believes it herself, that's just as bad."

Dad nodded.

"I just meant," Mia went on, "that it's not that easy to always know what you want, or whether it's sensible. Of course, no one wants to be *forced* into doing something. I think I know what I want, for instance, but I'm influenced."

"How?"

"I'm influenced by Mother's always preaching about how important it is for girls to get themselves an education and their own occupation and own money and not wreck their futures and all that. And obviously I'm influenced by the fact that I know I can't count on Mother's looking after the baby—like some other girls—anyway, I wouldn't dream of it.

"So it ought to be pretty easy for me to know what to do, I mean, and yet—and yet I'm brought up with a jerk, you see, when I think it'd be great to have a baby of my own . . . with Jan. And Jan says that we should get married and move in together, though I don't think he really wants to. He's only just qualified and he hasn't got a job. But he wants to do the right thing . . . and then he disapproves of abortion because he's influenced by *his* parents. Oh, goodness, what a mess it all is."

"And yet this discussion may well be quite theoretical."

"That's what Jan says—he doesn't even want to talk about it until he knows it's certain. But I said it was important whatever the facts are. You have to know what you want—once and for all. And it's terribly important to be able to talk about it. Oddly enough, you never seem to know what you really want until you've talked it out with someone else . . ." She fell silent, and then went on. "You know, it seems now that at last I do know what I want."

"But we won't say anything to Mother until you know definitely."

"Of course not."

There was a pause.

"Dad."

"Yes?"

"It was good being able to talk to you like this."

"Thanks, Mia dear."

He lifted her hand and kissed it.

"Wher*ever* have you *been*?" cried Lillan, rushing out into the hall when they opened the front door.

"We wrote you a note to tell you we'd gone for a drive and would stop for lunch somewhere," said Dad.

"Yes, I know, but you've been so long," said Mother, coming out of the kitchen with a plate in her hand. "We'd begun to think there'd been an accident."

"We got a bit late over lunch and the traffic was bad on the way back, and it was pretty slippery so we had to drive slowly."

"Where've you been?"

"At Sätra Guest House."

"Oh, Dad, I want to go to a restaurant with you, too," squealed Lillan, pulling at his arm.

"But you've just been to a two-day party and had a lovely time, haven't you?"

"Pelle was so silly all the time. He just wanted to fight. Though we had a lot of super food, and I got a Tyrolean hat with a feather in it and there was a fish pond and I got a notebook and a little baby doll. And today Pelle and Siv and I went out with Uncle Lasse and we went up the Kaknäs Tower and drank Cokes and ate buns. But Mother and Auntie Vera, they just sat at home talking and talking and talking."

"Come and eat now," said Mother.

"Eat," cried Mia. "I couldn't eat another thing today—we've already had pork and dessert and everything."

"You do look pale, darling," said her mother, coming up to her as she stood by the mirror, doing her hair. "Aren't you feeling well?"

She'd felt rather queasy even in the car, but she'd thought that was due to the fact that Dad was driving jerkily in the traffic. Perhaps they'd eaten too much rich food, she'd thought, and usually that awful strong coffee you get in restaurants didn't agree with her.

But her back ached too. Perhaps she'd sat too long on that jetty and caught a chill.

"As a matter of fact, I don't feel too good," she mumbled, looking appealingly at her mother. "I think I'll go to bed."

"Aren't you going to watch the long film?" said Lillan. "It says in the paper that it's really great."

"Go to bed, Mia dear, and I'll bring you a cup of tea and some toast later on," Mother said in a friendly way, patting Mia on the back.

As if someone had pressed a button, tears rose to Mia's eyes. "Oh, Mother, I'm so dreadfully tired," she would have liked to cry and then throw herself into her arms.

"I want tea and toast in bed too," complained Lillan. "You do look funny, Mia. Why are you just standing there staring?"

"I've got to go to the bathroom." Mia swiftly disappeared.

When she had locked the door behind her, she stood still again and held her hands over her stomach. Suddenly she felt something running down her leg, but she was incapable of doing anything except stand there, feeling that warm trickle. It was as if she were unable to grasp what had happened.

She sat down on the edge of the tub and slowly began to pull her pants off. A stream of dark red blood was trickling down one leg toward her ankle, sticking to her tights and collecting at her heel. So much . . . Oh, God.

It wasn't true. She sat as if numbed and just looked, unable to do anything about it, just staring and trying to recover from her shock. It had come. Exactly a month late. Crazy—she should be shouting with relief. But she had no energy to do anything.

She'd gone through all that hell . . . and then it had just come . . . she was almost angry, she felt so foolish.

Mechanically, she rolled down her tights and threw them on the floor with her pants. She took a towel and ran some warm water into the basin, feeling the pain in her stomach getting worse, spreading out across her back . . . oh, hell . . . it was so awful and what a mess. What if this were a—miscarriage? How did you know? And she didn't have any napkins at home . . . she'd run out ages ago and forgotten to buy more.

She hunted on her mother's shelf, but there weren't any there either. She couldn't very well go out and call now they were all sitting there eating.

God, the pain . . . she made a rough and ready napkin with a small towel.

I should be singing and dancing with delight.

Of course I'm glad. Everything's over, don't you understand? All that business of going to the abortion clinic and talking and explaining and telling Mother and convincing Jan and . . .

Suddenly she burst into tears, pressing another towel to her face to suppress the sounds, and then she sank down on the toilet seat and wept, wept from shock, wept from relief, wept from fatigue.

It was all so crazy.

Oh, God, if only she were in bed. She felt so exhausted that just the thought of getting to bed seemed almost too much. And how was she to fix the towel . . . were there any bandages . . . any safety pins? Mia didn't move to look, just sat there and let the tears fall.

It felt as if she had a huge leather sack of tears inside her that would go on falling forever and ever, and at the same time it was a comforting feeling in some way—letting everything run out of her, blood, tears, tension. Only now did she begin to realize the hideous anguish she'd been living with these last weeks.

It was strange that you survived, and yet . . . and yet it could have been worse. Think if Jan had been furious and had said she was to have it taken away. Then she would probably have reacted the other way, just because she didn't want to be made to do things.

And think of those girls who couldn't talk to their parents—who just went on and on although they *knew* they were pregnant and then had to have one of those horrible late abortions which they say are just as bad as a real birth.

And think if she'd been younger and not known what she had wanted at all.

Someone banged on the door. "Mia—telephone—it's Jan."

Help! She blew her nose. "I'm coming. Tell him I'm coming in a minute." She dragged on her pants and drank a glass of water. How would she be able to say a single sensible word—all messed up like this and sniveling?

She closed the kitchen door carefully before picking up the receiver and curling up in the corner of the sofa.

"Hi. No, I haven't got a cold. What sort of peculiar?" Mia struggled against her tears. "It's come—this evening. My period. Of course I'm pleased. Yes, of course, you can see that . . . though at the moment I'm dead beat. What? That's what you thought? Oh, I see. No, not tonight. Don't be crazy. I feel like hell. Yes, of course we must meet. Call me tomorrow, will you? Yes I *told* you I was pleased. But I've got such a foul stomachache. I'll stay at home from school tomorrow if it goes on like this, so call when you like. Oh, of course, I forgot to ask. How did it go? Did you win? Oh, good, an away match too. Do I sound grumpy? I'm not grumpy. Yes, I *have* been crying. Can't I cry if I want to, even if I am pleased? Yes, I'll probably be better tomorrow. Call then. 'By."

Mia lay in the dark in her room. She'd taken two aspirins and borrowed the electric blanket. The pains in her stomach had begun to slacken. The light was out but the blind was still up, the lights from the windows of the surrounding buildings floating out across the gardens and giving the room a mild indirect illumination which was restful and pleasing. Dad and Lillan had gone into the living room to watch a Jerry Lewis film and she could hear Lillan laughing in there. Her mother was walking backward and forward, doing things in the kitchen. There was a smell of coffee. Someone was talking on the neighbor's radio about the weather.

Everything was comfortingly as usual and yet at the same time quite different.

She felt so peculiar. She didn't understand.

Of course she was pleased—but not as she had expected, not so tremendously relieved and excited as you feel when you suddenly escape something horrible.

The relief seemed to have cost her so much . . . and taken so long to arrive that she couldn't experience it just like that with three rousing cheers and a hooray.

It was as if she would never again be as she had been before, childish like that, and unaware and credulous. Never, never ever again would she expose herself to this. Never. Never ever take a single risk again. That's what it felt like.

Was that how things worked—that you had to be terrified once first before you understood what it was really all about? Was that it? Was that why their sex education at school was so useless—not the fault of the teachers or the books or the timing or anything? Was it because it was just theory which went in one ear and out the other?

Think if girls like her and others who'd gone through this hell of waiting could stand up in class and say what it is really like in reality? Tell them what it's like to go around counting the days and hoping and doubting and not daring to go and *find* out. What it's like to try to find out exactly what you do want and what you don't. Going around waiting for the right moment to pour it all out to your parents . . . that it's a fearful responsibility whatever you do. Would it help? Would they believe her? Wouldn't they just grin and say, heavens, we know that as well as you do?

Does one always learn only from experience?

"Mia, are you asleep?"

Her mother was standing in the doorway with a tray. Mia switched on her bedside lamp.

"Well, how are you feeling?"

Mother put the tray down on a stool by Mia's bed and sat down in Gran's old white rocking chair, which Mia had inherited. "You do look green," she said. "Is it your period?"

Mia nodded. "It came in such a rush and I've got such awful cramps . . . I'm way overdue this time and it's always worse when it does come."

"Yes, it is," said her mother somewhat absently, rocking back and forth. "You've got the electric blanket, I suppose? Drink up your tea while it's hot."

"That's a nice dress," mumbled Mia as she munched her toast. "Red's nice with blond hair."

"Yes, it's a nice one," said her mother, stroking the front of the dress. It could be heard from her voice that her thoughts were elsewhere.

Mia drank her tea in silence. Funny that Mother hadn't asked her why she'd been crying. She couldn't believe that she'd been crying over a pain in her stomach. Perhaps she thought that Mia had been crying earlier on, over the separation. Perhaps she'd just never noticed. Her mother was sitting looking out of the window.

"Mia," she said finally. "I understand that Dad has spoken to you about . . . our plans?"

"Yes, he has."

"Actually we agreed to do it together, but he's just told me that it slipped out of him yesterday."

She sat silent again.

"Well," she asked then, a little impatiently. "What do you think?"

Mia swallowed violently.

"Um . . . I think that—it seems all right. I mean—of course, it's a pity, an awful pity . . . that you're separating . . ."

"It's a trial separation," interrupted Mother. "I think

that's the only way, you see, because as things are at the moment, it's impossible." She was rocking violently now.

"I see," Mia said tonelessly, ashamed that she couldn't feel more upset, but it was as if her store of feelings had in some strange way dried up for the moment, or become numbed. She simply hadn't the energy to set them free.

Although Mia was also lying looking out of the window, avoiding looking at her mother, she realized instinctively that her mother was disappointed by her reaction.

"I suppose Dad told you his version," she said after a while, slightly bitterly. "The first comer always has an advantage."

"He didn't do that at all," said Mia with sudden strength. "He just told me that you were going to do this and that you and Lillan were going to be in Halland this spring and we two here at home."

"And you haven't anything against that, have you, Mia? I mean . . . being alone with Dad here? He's promised . . ."

"It'll be fine!" Almost against her will, Mia put a little extra enthusiasm into her voice. The misery and rage of last night at the thought of her mother abandoning her seemed oddly distant.

"Oh, that's good, darling, that you've taken it so sensibly," her mother said, leaning over toward her. "I was so afraid that . . ." Again there was a slight tremor of disappointment in her voice.

"I've got Jan," said Mia.

"I'm glad you're friends again," her mother said, getting up from the rocking chair.

"So am I," said Mia.

It's not fair, thought Mia in despair. I should have told her everything. Now she'll never know what hell I've been through all this time. She's just occupied with her own miseries. Thinks I'm awful because I don't show more.

But Mia didn't say anything. She hadn't the energy. It was too late.

"Would you pull down the blind, please, Mother?" Mia said. "By the way, I'll probably stay at home tomorrow, if I feel the same."

"Of course you must do that." Her mother went over to the window. "Oh, yes," she went on, her back to Mia still, "apropos that, I thought of something . . . you've never asked me to help you with . . . contraceptives. Have you managed on your own?"

"No. I asked the school doctor once last year and he said I'm so irregular I shouldn't take the pill."

"Well, then we must . . . you must arrange something else, Mia," her mother said eagerly. "Promise me that . . . so that, so that nothing happens . . . unnecessarily, I mean. This new copper coil is supposed to be safe and harmless, I read in the paper. You can go to the clinic . . ."

"Don't worry, Mother. I'll go and arrange it myself as soon as I have time," Mia said, switching out the lamp. "Good night, and thanks for the tea."

"Good night, darling. Hope you sleep it all off."

She ran her hand over Mia's feet under the blanket as she walked toward the door. Neither of them looked at each other.

"Mother!" Mia called just as the door was closing. "Ask

Dad to come in and say good-night when the movie's over, will you? I won't go to sleep before then."

She had completely forgotten that her father didn't know what had happened. It seemed unnecessary for him to worry about that as well as everything else, especially if he had to sleep on that uncomfortable sofa in the living room again tonight.

Mia didn't have to make an effort to stay awake as she lay waiting for her father, although the light was out, and it wasn't just the pain in her stomach that kept her from sleeping.

It must be like this to be grown up, she thought.

It wasn't just that things were different from what you had thought, but also your own feelings and reactions became unexpected and frightening.

You couldn't be really glad, although you should.

You couldn't really grieve over the separation, which only a month ago would have been a catastrophe.

She suddenly didn't know whether it was love she'd felt so strongly for Jan when they'd been sitting in front of the fire. After the telephone call tonight he'd become strangely unreal. He'd just gone on about how glad she should be that everything was over, all their problems solved—no threatening unpleasantness, no conscience troubles. His father's God had been good and rewarded him because he'd been loving and just and offered marriage and protection.

But why was she thinking like this—why was she being so nasty? She was fond of him, wasn't she? She'd been glad when he'd said he wanted to get married, even if she herself had never thought that . . . why was she so irritated when he began to talk about all the goals they'd got at the handball match? Wasn't he allowed to be pleased now all his troubles were over? So that they could begin again and go to the discotheque and to bars and walk in the park and sleep together in the little room in Björk Street.

And why had she been so strange with Mother this evening, withdrawing and unable to make the effort, seeming to take sides with Dad and apparently not even upset, although the whole of her felt like a great sore inside?

Oh, God, it felt so horrible.

Mia sat up in bed and covered her face with her hands.

It was as if she'd never before understood what the word anguish meant.

This irrational incomprehensible pounding black anguish which made you feel as if you were going mad.

It's because I'm so tired. It's my period. It'll pass it'll pass it'll pass . . . oh . . . it must pass.

The door opened slowly.

"Dad!" It sounded like a cry for help although she hadn't meant it to.

"I was only going to say good-night . . . you asked. Don't you feel well?"

"Oh, Dad, come over here."

He went over to her bed and stood silently and expectantly in the dark.

"I just wanted to tell I got my period."

"I guessed as much."

He sat down on the edge of her bed and she found his hand.

"That undoubtedly solves a lot of problems," he said gently.

"But, Dad." Mia's voice was shaking a bit. "Dad, I don't understand. It's so horrible. I feel so peculiar, you see. Of course I'm glad. Of course. But at the same time . . . at the same time it's as if I couldn't summon up the energy to be glad. I just want to cry. Everything's such an awful mess."

"That's probably quite natural, Mia. It's often like that when you've gone around in a great state of tension and then suddenly it lets go. You get a kind of shock, I think, a kind of backlash. You haven't really any idea how great the tension has been until afterward."

"In fact I feel absolutely ghastly," whispered Mia, letting the tears come again.

"I recognize that."

"*You* do?"

"I've felt like that many a time, Mia dear, many a time, and I know it'll pass after a while, but that doesn't make it any better while it lasts."

Mia lay silently and felt her father's hard dry hand around her sweaty fingers. The tears ran into her half-open mouth and tasted of salt.

"It feels good to hear . . . that someone else . . ."

"It's always good to know that you're not alone in your . . . reactions," said her father.

"But Jan. He doesn't understand that! When I spoke to him on the phone just now he didn't seem to be able to grasp that I wasn't deliriously happy and yelling and screaming with delight."

"You'll have to try to tell him. That's probably the only way to get people to understand. To try to explain to them. How could they know otherwise?"

"But you knew."

"Jan's so young."

"Yes, he's very young . . . he really is."

"But he can't help that, can he?"

"No, that's true," said Mia with a giggle. Then she lay still and silent again, staring out into the dark and at her father's silhouette against the bright line coming through the kitchen door.

"I feel better now, Dad," she said, in the end.

"That's good, Mia."

ABOUT THE AUTHOR

Gunnel Beckman lives in Solna, Sweden, with her husband. The mother of five children, she edited the women's page of a daily newspaper in Gothenberg and has worked as a probation officer. Ms. Beckman has written a number of books for young people, two of which have appeared in English, *Admission to the Feast* and *A Room of His Own.*